Sinners Circle

This book is dedicated to my mother, Vanita Sims. I love you.

sinners circle

©2017
6th Finger Press

No, I ain't scared of lightening,
And the thunder never killed,
I was born in a summer storm,
I live there still
-Tom Mcrae

Chapter 1

I was born in the summertime, inside a house inside a storm. The winds and quakes were so bad, mom said, they had to loop rope through the handles on the cabinets to keep the dishes from spilling onto the floor. My Aunt Marcy wrapped duct tape on all the black plated chandeliers, said they looked like shiny wasp nests swinging this way and that. They locked all the windows, pushed bookcases over the tall ones in case the glass broke and shot across the room like sparkling shrapnel.

My mother told me she and Marcy were in the living room playing cribbage, drinking hot chocolate and keeping their candles low in case anyone passing through the long stretches of wheat fields came close enough to notice the house they were holed up in. They were playing cribbage and it doesn't matter who was winning because somewhere in either the middle or the end my mother's water broke. At first the two of them just stared at the puddle under the chair, the wet spreading in my mother's jeans until she bucked forward. Her mouth gaping, eyes closed, she knocked the cribbage board onto the floor, fingers clawed out towards Marcy.

And then the storm started. Between contractions my mother was shuffling through the house pushing forgotten furniture that wasn't hers across dusty rooms that belonged to no one.

Even with all the windows blocked and exits sealed my aunt was still nervous. In between telling my fifteen-year old mother to push, she would get up from between her shaking, pencil thin legs and peek through tiny holes in the furniture piled in front of the windows. "What if someone's coming?"

My mother said she couldn't remember much of that night. She kept blacking out, waking up soaked in sweat, her head in Marcy's lap. At some point, just before I came out, she said she came to for a moment. Marcy was across the room, back against the front door, hugging her knees and crying beneath that polished wasp nest that swung slow and steady as a pendulum. After that, she said all she could remember was me in her arms and how it took half an hour for Marcy to work up the nerve to cut the umbilical cord. She kept crying and picking up and putting down the kitchen knife saying things like, "What if I kill her? What if I hurt her? What if she dies and it's *my* fault?"

I wasn't a big baby. My mom being so young at the time and on the run with her little sister, without a doctor to tell her, it was several years later that she discovered I was three weeks premature.

When I was six, every night she ended the story with, "But I knew when I looked at your tiny face, and you opened those big blue eyes, you were my little girl." My mother would squeeze me inside my bed, flick the lights off and blow me a kiss. "I love you, sweetheart." When she shut the skinny four panel door, I'd crawl out of bed and look through the honeycomb shades, my eyes sweeping the rest of the trailers in the park, looking through windows into other people's lives. I'd watch the teenagers kiss and feel each other up on the baseball field I could only see half of from my window. I'd listen to the sounds of radios and arguments and car engines turning over, and the constant drone of night insects. I'd do this until I heard the TV in the living room turn off, my mom phoning somebody, leaving a message, hanging up. I'd wait fifteen minutes after I heard her pull out the cot and stop shifting around on the springs, and then I'd open my door, tip toe down the hallway and crawl in beside her. Even when she was drunk, mom kissed my hair and sang to me. Twinkling stars, mockingbirds, black sheep. I'd fall asleep with the smell gin and stale cigarette smoke in my nostrils, but 'you are my sunshine, my only sunshine' in my ears and my hands pressed against my mother's heart.

Chapter 2

Karl, he's waving a picture of Marilyn Monroe in my face. His labored breathing and the crunching sound of the paper barely muffles the sound of somebody moaning in the next room as they pinch off a heavy shit in the toilet. "According to Maria, this is the devil."

Marilyn's paper face folding and unfolding as she flaps between Karl's fingers, it's like she's blowing air under my eyelids.

"Maria said Marilyn would whisper stuff to her while she was sleeping. Like, she would make Maria get up and do shit. She wound up in this place..." His finger circles the ceiling. "...after she walked through a sliding glass door at 3am. Neighbors found her covered in blood, passed out on their lawn."

He leans in close, his lips barely on my cheek, his eyes aimed straight up, "Marilyn Monroe made Maria eat her own dog."

He slaps the photo down onto the wooden desk he's leaning against. Its surface is carved up with so many little swastikas and curly *FUCK YOU*'s, I'm surprised it doesn't cave in like balsawood when Karl raps his knuckles all over the 'SATAN' and 'PUSSY' gashes.

He pulls a dusty Sony Watchman off the shelf, one of those portable TV sets you don't see anymore, and wags it in my face. "Steven thought

Jesus was talking to him through this thing. He thought God was televising His messages. See this?" He slides a finger over the 'Watchman' logo. "He thought it, literally, meant 'watch man'. With this hunk of junk, Steve thought he was a Shepard of men."

Karl slams it on the table, hard, and reaches for a hamster wheel. "This made Greg think he could punish his enemies. He would buy hamsters, take them home and watch them run on it. After a few hours, he'd burn the little beasts so the cops couldn't find any evidence in case the person he was trying to kill, did actually *die*."

I take the wheel from Karl, slip my fingers in and out of the little spaces between the wires. "How'd he get in here?"

"Pet shop owner called the ASPCA after his eleventh hamster. When someone came poking around, they found crushed snakes nailed all around his door frame. He wound up attacking the poor ASPCA gal with a garden rake. Really fucked up one of her arms, I guess."

The toilet flushes in the other room so I don't quite hear Karl when he says something about Greg having raccoon fur glued to his armpits when he got here.

"I'm gonna take this stuff home with me when they get discharged, add it to the collection."

He takes the hamster wheel away from me, plugs his finger through the middle and spins it a little. I try cracking my neck, but nothing happens.

He leans against the tin shelves that are sagging under the weight of all the piled junk. Karl tosses the hamster wheel onto the table and tents his fingers, "I gotta go do rounds in a few minutes. You can wait in the common room for me if you want, but I'll be an hour, maybe less."

I nod, follow him out the little storage room and past the men's bathroom. We go down this real shabby looking hallway, the carpet is so worn down you can see the cement flooring coming through in some places. At the end of the hallway we go through this steel door with a

Sinners Circle

grated window, which takes us through the residence quarters. Each little room has its own metal door, clipboards dangling from yarn tied through the wire windows. It's eerie because on one side almost everybody is weeping, on the other side, you can literally hear patients screaming and their jaws grinding. That awful sound of tooth on tooth echoing loud as their socked feet slam the bolted bed frames, the noise following you in tiny booms down the corridor.

Karl takes me into the main lobby and says he'll be back in a bit. He says if I need anything, just talk to the nurse at the office and "...make sure you show her your visitor's pass."

I sit down on this huge floral couch and reach for a magazine as Karl disappears around a corner.

I'm leafing through issues of Anchor, SZ, Black And White, Cosmopolitan, Mental Health Today when this fat guy comes shuffling up to me and says, "They keep Archies in the library."

"Library?"

He points a sausage finger at a table, the steel legs wrapped in electrical tape. There's three Granny Smith Apple boxes half full of assorted reading material, and when I dig through them, they consist mainly of motel Bibles and Jughead Double Digests. I grab one were Jughead is dressed like a mummy on the front cover, telling a cute pirate girl that his favorite type of music is 'wrap.' I walk back to the couch but the fat guy is sitting in my spot, staring into space, a look of total despair spreading almost instantly across his face.

I sit at the very end of the couch, scratch my crotch and wonder if Karl will be back sooner than he said. Ethel is wrapping her arms around Jughead who is clearly unpleased when the fat guy at the other end of the couch starts crying. I look at the clock and know that if he keeps crying, within five minutes a nurse will come. I know that within eight minutes she'll go back into her little office and within ten minutes she'll be feeding him Ativan. Within twelve minutes I can be in the coma ward and within thirteen minutes I can be inside a patient's room with the door locked behind me.

But only if the fat man keeps crying. If he stops, the nurse won't come. If he isn't crying I won't be able to get into the coma ward. Funny thing about this hospital is, there are only two ways to enter the coma ward. One is by elevator, which requires special authorization codes. That and there are video surveillance cameras above the button panel. Sure, I could keep my head down, but eventually I would be caught. Not to mention, I imagine the code is subject to change as well, and clearly, I am not hospital personnel.

The only other method of entry would be right through that door beside the nurses' station. The coma ward functions in accordance with the psychiatric ward, which I am inside right now. This is a special psych ward though, in the sense that this ward specializes almost exclusively in psychotics. When one of the patients here undergoes some kind of massive mental breakdown, they dope them up and wheel them into the coma ward for a couple a days. What it boils down to is, Karl is rubbing elbows with the hardcore psychotics and inner-city lunatics who wind up getting shipped to this very special floor. He's checking beds every fifteen minutes to make sure no one has swallowed their tongue or caved their skull in against the wall, he's checking to see that they haven't sliced their wrists on the wall vents or punctured an artery while digging imaginary microchips out of their arms or thighs. He is fishing clothing out of the toilets, tightening arm restraints, and assuring anxious patients that nobody is following them, that nobody is listening in. He is scrubbing piss off the walls and taking home their memorabilia.

I've known Karl for a good eight years now, and he's worked here for seven of those. When we first met, we were both at a lesbian bar. We were laughing at the same drag queen and he wound up taking home the girl I was going to murder that night. I guess he started dating this waitress Alison who works at a coffee shop a few stores down from the porn store

I'm working at. The two of them came in one night looking for a blow-up sheep for a friend's birthday party. He weaseled his way into my life like that and it was painfully embarrassing to be friends with a guy. I'd considered slitting his throat when he invited me on a hike, but when I saw Alison get in the car I knew it wouldn't happen. When I discovered he worked here, I thought it would be good fun to come poke at the psychotics; that is until I discovered the coma ward. When I discovered he worked here, I started returning his phone calls. I started inviting him over for beers and I started laughing at his stupid jokes. The other night he clapped me on the back and said, "Amanda, you're the closest friend I've ever had." We were doing shots and flicking quarters at strippers, I was heating mine with a lighter. "You're not 'core like me, but you understand that maybe I'm just a lot different than the rest of the world. Thanks."

I flipped a quarter down the poster funnel a stripper was holding over her landing strip. She yelped and looked around, whistled the bouncer over and pointed at the two guys in front of me. I looked at Karl as the bouncer hauled the two dudes away and smiled as we took their seats, but I wasn't smiling because of him. He grinned back and ran a hand through his faggy emo hair.

Back on the couch, the fat man puts his head down to his knees, rocking himself a little. From out the nurse's station, the biggest but-her-face comes skipping over with a meds cup. She's soothing the big dummy as I slip through the coma ward door, wave my visitors pass in a passing orderly's direction and walk up and down the hallways, peering in at the sleeping patients.

Depending on what you want to do, it's best to find a patient who's already covered in cuts and burns. It's best to find a woman who's already bruised up, so new handprints won't seem so unusual, though I'm sure for research purposes this really fucks up the healing statistics.

I stop outside the room of a girl whose face is covered in bandages, strands of blonde hair poking through the top. I laugh, thinking about the

Jug Head Digest, all wrapped up like a mummy, talking to the sexy pirate. I look up and down the hallway, it's totally clear, so I slip inside, lock the door and roll the little curtain down over the window. I stand there for a few seconds, take off my jacket and pick up the clipboard swinging at the foot of the bed. Marianne Pollanski DOB: May 7, 1993, injured in a car accident, multiple bone fractures, lacerations to the stomach and pelvis from dashboard, second-degree burns on the face, thighs and calves from explosion of vehicle gas tank. Highlighted at the bottom are the words: Condition: critical/unstable. ATTN Nurse: Sophia Harris.

I put the clipboard down and sit on the edge of her bed.

Up on the window ledge are flowers, decorated helium proclaiming 'Happy birthday,' 'Get well soon' cards and pictures of teenagers jumping on a trampoline, a little blonde girl smiling so big her eyes are closed. I roll the covers down to get a look at her legs. They look like two yellow banana peppers cooked over a campfire. Unopened birthday presents stacked on the floor, a rugby jersey and field hockey stick laid carefully out on a chair beside a breathing machine. I look from the pictures, down to the girl wrapped up in this bed, barely alive. Poor little Marianne.

I breathe heavy, put her little hand in mine. I stroke the puffy skin and give her fingers a gentle squeeze. I get up, pick some lint off her tiny jersey and turn her field hockey stick over in my hands. I trace my fingers over the smooth wood and turn to Marianne, laughing a little, "You any good?"

I smile when she doesn't answer. "So modest. You're so modest, Marianne." I try balancing the stick on my palm and walk over to the window, look at a picture of a smiling boy, Marianne piggy backing on top of him.

"You think he'll still go down on you?" I point the stick at her legs and chuckle.

I try cracking my neck again and when nothing happens I check my watch. If this hospital's employees aren't on smoke breaks, I have eight minutes. I flex my grip on the stick with both hands and yank off her covers.

Chapter 3

"Don't bother alphabetizing any of the DVDs. Most of these newer titles start with A's anyway." My boss Blaine, is fanning himself with a couple films in his big gorilla palms. *"Ass-stimulation, Asian Anal Amateur, Annie Chokely, All American Amateur* parts six and seven... so you just put them up according to date, see?" He pushes a stack of movies into my arms and says, "I'll be in my office."

This means he'll be in the janitor's closet. The one he tore the sink out of and put a desk and table lamp in. The safety shower is still there, but it's stuffed full of mangled dildos and punctured bottles of flavored lubricant. He's got skin rags with torn covers stacked five feet high in there.

I nod, trying not to drop any DVDs. "Sure."

When he leaves, I look at the hundreds of movies spilling out of the stacked boxes all around me. I'm literally surrounded by enough porn to keep the TV on for a decade. Funny thing is though, when you spend hours handling pornography, you start to think about things like grocery lists. You wonder if you're brushing your teeth enough, you consider whether or not to get a pet and weigh heavy the pros and cons of having said animal. Your hands on top of Jesse Jane's tits your thinking, "Am I getting enough absorbency from my current brand of toilet paper?" Staring down the holes of topless teenage lesbians you wonder if you are getting enough fiber from your breakfast cereal. There's a certain desensitization that takes place when you spend all day with dicks and tits in your face. Though every once in a while, and I mean *rarely*, you come across something that either cracks you up or gets those greasy wheels of sex turning round in your mind.

For instance, I'm almost done shelving all these movies, I'm sliding a copy of *Pushing the Pink* onto the rack and I notice the two girls on the cover. By industry standards they are two normal blonde babes, tits in hand, arching their backs in an attempt to look skinnier, but the thing that catches my eye are the two humungous dicks strapped over their slits. This isn't anything new, for Christ's sake we sell strap-ons here and even move a couple each week. But these girls, these two twits gripping their tits on the cover of this DVD, they've got that look like they've been rode hard and put away wet, but the life in their eyes now, when they've got these big plastic penises belted around their pussies, it's staggering.

    According to Freud, the penis wasn't just the man's erotic zone; it was the *sole* erotic zone. Period. Freud assumed the characterization of women was only noting their differences from men. He coined the phrase, "Women are castrated." See, according to Freud women must sense some kind of inferiority to men because nature dictates females as *incomplete beings*. This is where the masculinity complex comes into play because once a woman is made aware of the wound to her narcissism, she develops a scar on her ego. So, she starts to share the contempt felt by men for a sex which is of less importance and thus, insists on being just like the average run of the mill asshole guy on the street. Because, clearly, it's not enough to be fucked, but to be the one fucking that gives you the power. There have been thousands of women in the Adult Film Industry who try and defy this role assigned to their gender. These girls, they insist on being *the stud* and rearranging the order of 'dominance.' But in the end, it never pans out and they just wind up being real paid whores who make a couple bucks whilst setting the feminist movement back again and again with this awful defiance of logic. Never the less, this whole super sexed thing on camera is bound to take its emotional toll on the lesser successful starlets, such as these two girls on the cover of *Pushing the Pink*. This is a total bummer because strictly speaking from a dermatological aspect, stress is a real skin killer and looking at these two girls, they got stress coming out the wazoo. Late rent buried deep in their eyelids. Bounced checks burrowed into their foreheads. They've got high school dropout stamped into their laugh lines. But their eyes, their eyes have that same look people on TV have when they win the lottery. They've got the same look as a fat kid given unlimited access to the Hershey's factory. Now, right now with their cunts hidden, huge rubber cocks strapped over top, they look happier then you've ever seen them before. They're beaming like pregnant Mormon newlyweds.

    I flip the case over and see a bunch of queeny boys on the back. They're fish facing and posing as slutty as the girls ever could. I smile thinking how cute the whole concept of women trying to fuck men is. I think it's totally great that for one day they got to be the ones drilling holes and pounding ass. Makes me think of a Make-a-Wish Foundation for used up porn stars dying of AIDS and the advanced stages of various STDs and the kinds of wishes they'd make. "I'd like to shoot my dad," or, "I'd like to rape *my* brother while *my* friends watch." You know, that kind of thing. I laugh a little and put the DVD on the shelf, turn around and almost smash into this guy standing right behind me.

    He's got real shaggy grey hair and those huge black sun blockers that only sex perverts and old people wear and he's hugging a packaged blow up doll to his chest. He's got a whale of a waist line, the pockets of his green khakis bulging like huge tumors. He stands a whole two heads taller than me and when he doesn't move out of the way I wonder how much blood is in his body. "I'm ready to make a purchase."

    I walk over to the till and scan his doll while he runs his fingers through the display of dangling keychain whips on the counter. I stuff the doll inside a small garbage bag and make sure our fingers don't touch as he hands me three twenties. I slide him his change across the counter, "Is that everything?"

    He nods, mumbles something to himself on his way out, his pockets swaying massive. A couple feet from the doors he stops real awkwardly, and looks at the lingerie display on the wall. When he steps between the two security poles by the door the sound of the alarm is almost deafening.

This big lug, he spins around to face me, pushes his hands in his pockets and pulls out foam tit stress balls, vibrating penis pens, a miniature pocket pussy. Handfuls of flavored condoms, little vibrators and bottles and bottles of heating lubricant fly onto the floor. The look on his face, he looks like a deer caught in headlights. I kind of just stand there and then sit down on my stool. After a few seconds, when I do nothing but sort of tent my fingers and think about buying different toilet paper, he yells at the top of his lungs, "Only God can judge me!" then runs out the door, his mouth hung open, that fucking garbage bag blow up doll held tight against his chest.

Chapter 4

If I squint and look at the park benches sideways, they look like tombstones in the dark. The only light comes from the moon and a few dim lamps lined along the jogging path far enough apart from one another to create a space of total darkness before one ends and another begins. I'm sucking the shells of the M&Ms so thin that when I rattle them between my teeth, they shatter and make me think of cave men kneeling in sand, beating dry animal bones over rock. From where I'm standing I can see the jogging path but not much of it. My view is skewed by trees grown together in thick clusters and if I enter this tiny forest, I can reach the back door of my house within minutes.

Out of the corner of my eye I can see dim shadow play, slight changes in the light on the path. I slip into the trees, branches dragging across my face, past my ears. About twenty feet in, I'm across from the water fountain and from here I can see the path in its entirety. From here I can see as the little dirt route winds slightly, making the runner zig zag as they make their way down. I pop more M&Ms in my mouth, rattle them around and smile as I watch the person swerve closer.

I can see she's female. As she moves in and out from under the lamps I see that she's wearing a white t-shirt, white ear buds attached to an iPod strapped to her arm, brown hair pulled back into a ponytail, swinging back and forth with every sprint. I wouldn't call her fat, but I wouldn't call her beautiful either. She's not skinny enough to be actually pretty. When she's close to the fountain she slows down to a walk. Across her chest her shirt reads *University of Oklahoma*.

Out of nowhere, another jogger appears from the other direction and this one has a dog. Her pace indicates she doesn't intend on stopping to have a drink, but her dog stops in mid run, turning in my direction and barking, barking, barking. He's up on both hind legs barking at the face he can't see. The woman, she slaps her dog on the back, yanks his leash and drags him along with her. He doesn't stop barking and she doesn't stop jogging. The things people will ignore for a good cardio workout.

The lady with the dog disappears, leaving *University of Oklahoma* alone in the dark. She stretches her legs when she stops, panting she wipes some loose hair off her forehead, her hands on her hips as she steps awkwardly towards the fountain. I'm guessing that she probably moved up here after school, got a new job, a new boyfriend, started some new life. Jogging must be her way of feeling like she's really holding it together, like she's doing well for herself because she's staying active and eating right. Even with her head in the fountain, she doesn't take out her ear buds as she laps up quick gulps of water. Looking up and down the path to make sure no one is near, I'm winding a stretch of nylon cord around my knuckles, a length of two and a half feet give or take, stroking the sides with my thumb, making sure it's nice and tight. I close my eyes for just that second when I hear her come up for air, gasping, a throat full of water about to shoot down into her belly. I move out of the trees, across the grass, the path and dirt silent as a ghost, the cord twice around her neck faster than she can flinch. Before her hands shoot up I've turned her around so she's facing the woods. I kneel into her spine and she drops hard on her face. I stand up fast, yanking the cord so she has no option but to stand with me or choke to death right there. A few steps forward is all it takes and she's collapsed into the brush and trees of the little forest. Just before I feel her go completely limp, before the lights go out, I flip her over and her knee sails weak into my crotch. This is learned behavior; I guess being dragged into the bushes must not be a new thing for her. But when she sees my long hair, feels the flatness where, statistically speaking, the dick of an abductor should be, I don't *need* to slam her skull against the trunk of a tree because she just passes out trying to scream with whatever air is still inside of her lungs. I don't *need* to do it, but I do anyways.

Sims

Sticks and branches snapping beneath her weight, my sneakers, I drag her by the armpits into the basement of my house. My basement, it's actually just a tiny root cellar with old wood floors and chairs that I have to keep replacing because of chop marks. I keep these chairs held in place with steel brackets and a couple of screws. However, before I can really get her down there, she starts to wake up and I don't want to fall down the stairs along with her when she starts flailing and kicking up a storm, so I just let her go, her body tumbling down the steps. I close the basement door and turn on the light at the top of the stairs before going down to her. There's a big split on her hair line, blood trails running through her hair and down both cheeks. I put my head to her chest, my fingers on her wrist to make sure she's still alive, that she's still with me. Puny bumps under my middle and pointer finger tell me I haven't lost her yet. I strip off her clothes and sit her up on the chair; I loop one hand through the back and lock her wrists with handcuffs. Same story with the ankles, only I spread her legs apart and cuff them at the back.

Sometimes I like to make movies, that's why I keep camera equipment down here, but mostly I just like to take pictures—pictures with tons of flash; women tend to scream more when there's lots of flash, especially if I've turned off the lights. Tonight, I take off my clothes, toss them onto the stairs and switch on the power strip my video camera is plugged into. While I wait a few seconds for it to turn on I look behind me, at the axe against the wall, the hunting knife hanging on a nail. This camera of mine, it's one of those old school VHS deals, great as long as you don't have to use the battery pack. Outdoors it's hopeless; the battery only runs for five minutes, even if you spend three days charging the crap out of it. Karl gave it to me about three years ago. It was signed into the psych ward inventory and swiped a couple days later. Karl and I, we'd been talking about shooting some wedding videos on the side. Well, more so him than me. He said something about wanting to capture unhappy faces at celebrations or some retarded thing. He spent thirty bucks running an ad in the newspaper and when he finally got a call back, the soon-to-be newlyweds sent him packing when they caught a glimpse of his equipment. So he gave it to me, and I've been using it ever since.

I sit behind the camera and massage my pussy till it's good and wet enough to slip a few fingers in and out of. I do this for a good five minutes before *University of Oklahoma*, her head bowed to her chest, wakes up and blinks for a few seconds. I didn't notice it before, but one of her eyes has gone totally red and the lid doesn't open all the way. Her head is swaying from one side of the tiny room to the other, totally dazed, when I smile at her and say "Hi."

Her head slowly bobbing in my direction, she stares dead center into the camera and screams when she sees me propped up on my knees, pushing fingers into myself. My aunt Marcy, she lives two floors up from this little basement, and she's half deaf and in a wheelchair. There isn't a ramp for her to take down to my floor, the one below hers, so I don't really have to worry about any interruptions. Nevertheless, even coming from a throat that is probably bruised and will swell shut by morning, this girl is screaming pretty damn loud. That's because fear, *real* fear will make you do things you'd think you couldn't do. I'm pretty sure if those handcuffs weren't the real deal, she'd break right through them. She screams when I walk on my knees towards her. She screams when I dip my head between her thighs and she screams the whole ten minutes I spend licking her pussy and chewing her tits. She keeps yelling, "What the *fuck* are you doing?" She keeps yelling, "*Stop* it!" Even when her voice is hoarse and all scratchy she keeps calling for help.

When I start getting bored, I sit on her lap, wrap my arms around her shoulders, she tries to spit in my face but there isn't anything in her mouth but strings of blood and strips of tissue from biting her tongue and inner cheek. She can't look me in the eyes, she kind of just bows her head and whimpers, "Why are you doing this?"

I want to hug her but I don't want to get within head butting range. I drum my fingers on her shoulder and pull her hair so she has to look in my face, but she keeps her eyes closed so I pull hard at one of her earlobes until she opens them. I smile, stroking the side of her head, the one I whacked against the tree. "Look, I'll tell you what, okay? If you..." I tap her tit with my fingertip, "...if *you* suck my cunt for about, oh let's say five minutes..." Her eyes start to close and her head slumps down a bit. I pull her hair again, tears rolling from her swollen eyes. I hold up my hand, all five fingers wide apart, "Just *five* minutes and I'll let you go. I absolutely swear..." I put my hand over where my heart is supposed to be. "I will let you out of the handcuffs. Okay?"

We sit there, her cuffed to that chair, me on her lap, we just *sit* there in total silence until her head drops, I can't tell if it's her throat that's finally ballooning up or if it's real pain in her voice when she finally speaks. "*Why* are you *doing* this?"

I pinch her cheeks, squint into her eyes and can't stop myself from grinning into her adorable little face, baby talking and everything. "Because you're just *so cute!*"

I stand up, put my leg up on her thigh and push my pussy into her face. In a situation like this, one that already seems impossible to imagine, a victim will always believe escape *is* possible. No one wants to believe they are about to die when just an hour before they were doing something as normal as going for a jog. No one wants to accept that just one hour later they are locked inside a dark, grubby basement, tied to a chair and suffering from massive head trauma while being forced to perform oral sex on some pale lesbian.

University of Oklahoma, the silly, stupid girl, she takes a sort of deep breath and goes for the plunge. I can tell right away it's her first time doing this. Clearly, she didn't do much experimenting in college and right now, her performance level is proof. But the good news is, eating pussy is not a science, it's *not* difficult. In fact, I'm willing to gamble that it's one of the easiest things known to man, because after a little bit, she's doing great.

Those five minutes I promised, well they go right out the window. I'm guessing I make her do this for a good fifteen to twenty before I come and pull away. "See? That wasn't so hard, was it?"

She looks away, shivers and spits off to the side. "Can I go now? My boyfriend..." Her eyelids opening and closing separately, she's slurring her words. "...he'll worry." I'm not sure if she can feel it, but there's a steady stream of blood running out of her right ear. I'm trying to focus on what she's saying, but the flow of blood is very distracting.

I stand up, nod, walk back behind the camera. I make sure the shot is still dead center, and it is. "Yeah, you can go now."

Her shoulders sag in relief.

I bend over, look into the eye piece of the camera and reach behind me, grabbing the axe leaning against the wall. "Thing is..." Her eye lids, they blink out of synch just as her other ear begins to hemorrhage large drops of crimson onto her neck and chest. "Thing *is* babe, I don't have any keys for those cuffs." I stand up straight. "But I said I'd get you out of those right? And fair's fair."

Her eyes bulge as the axe catches her collar bone. She screams so loud I don't even hear the bones snap.

I laugh. "Oops! Sorry sweetheart, *I missed*!"

Hot ribbons of blood whip across my face, my stomach, my whole body as I swing again, taking off her arm at the elbow. With three chops, one of her legs comes loose above the kneecap. She only stops screaming when the axe opens the bottom of her throat and top of her sternum. I slip the cuffs off the hands on the floor. I light a cigarette, turn off the camera, eject the tape and toss it onto her lap. "You can go home to your boyfriend now."

Chapter 5

"Yeah that's true, so does The Beatles' 'Revolution Number 9.' Played backwards the words are 'turn me on dead man turn me on dead man.' Crazy shit, huh?" Karl pushes the neck of his beer bottle into his chest and scratches his nose. Turning to the guy sitting beside him, the guy wearing brown leather everything, bright pink sunglasses *inside* the club, Karl nudges him and says, "Stairway to Heaven, I think goes something like, 'there was a little tool shed where he made us suffer sad Satan.'"

The leather man, his drink clinks against mine as he lifts it off the table, up to his lips. "Gotta think about it, man. Led Zeppelin, man. They knew what they were writing..."

I take a swig of my beer, try cracking my neck as I look over at a blonde waitress who once told me she was a model or something. I put the bottle back on the table and inch over a bit towards Alison, who looks about as bored as I am. "Well you'd think that, but Zeppelin technically never *wrote* 'Stairway to Heaven.'" Karl rolls his eyes and shifts in his seat as I lift my beer again. "It was actually written by a band called Spirit in nineteen sixty-seven. Spirit toured with Zeppelin but the band kinda fizzled out and Zeppelin just stole it from them."

Karl and the leather man are quiet for a minute, then leather man says, "'They give him a six, six, six.'"

I shake my head, "No, it's 'He'll give those with him six, six, six.'"

Leather man heaves a sigh, "They didn't *steal* it from Spirit." He stands up and staggers off towards the dance floor, his feet vanishing inside a cloud of fog being sprayed into a mob of dancing drunken nobodies.

Alison is peeling the label off her beer. Karl kisses her shoulder and runs a hand through his hair. "I hate *Chambers*. Why do we always come here?"

I shrug and chug my beer. Karl laughs at nothing, like an idiot but, Alison doesn't. She keeps peeling the paper label off the beer she isn't drinking. She scowls at me, "You know this is a gay bar, right?"

The waitress-model-blonde girl, whatever she is—she's all legs anyway—she winks at me as she walks by holding a tray of pints and shot glasses gleaming like razor blades. I smile and sip my drink, turning away from her, looking at Alison. "Well, no *shit*. Really?"

She rolls her eyes, quickly looking at Karl, at me, back at her peeled bottle. I point at it. "It's a sign of frustration, you know."

Alison's head doesn't move when she looks at me. "What?"

It's hard to hear with all this music so I lean in. "What?"

"What?"

"What are you talking about?"

She tears a big strip off the glass, rolls it between her fingers. "What's what?"

I lean in closer. "*What*?"

She rolls her eyes again. The song playing, a bad remix of some top forty sensation cuts out as she shouts, "What's a sign of *frustration*?"

Her whole face goes red as about twenty people turn and look at her. Another rotten club mix comes pounding out of the speakers as I lean back into the padding of our tiny semi-circle booth. "Peeling the labels off your drink." I flick a tiny ball of paper off the table.

Karl laughs and pokes her in the ribs, "Yeah I heard this somewhere. They say it's a sign of sexual tension. You aren't sexually frustrated, are you, babe?"

She glares at him. "Says *who*? *Who* says it's a sign?" He shrugs and drinks his beer, his glassy eyes wandering over to the dance floor where two skinny girls with pixie cuts are kissing each other.

I tap the table with two fingers. "Well to be fair, it's a sign of anxiety, really. And anxiety is believed to be released through sexual intercourse. So, put two and two together and bingo, you've got a common misconception."

"What?" She smirks, biting her nails.

"Do you want me to tell you about how they used to deal with anxious women in the nineteen twenties?"

She shakes her head, spits a few nail fragments onto her jeans, the table. A fleck of white lands on my wrist, when she brushes it away her fingers are wet and when she sees she's got spit on my hand she looks like she's about to cry. I smile and rub the back of my hand clean on her jeans, her thighs clench when I touch her and looking at her face I notice that she's only wearing one earring. "You okay?"

Karl looks back from the dance floor, at her, at me. "She's okay. We did a bunch of blow earlier. I think the shit was cut with something bad because she's been acting like this since we got here."

Her mouth twitches as she says. "No, I haven't."

He flicks a wad of Alison's label at me. "Well, since *you* got here anyway." He takes a slow drink of beer.

I look at Alison, she looks down at her lap and then back at Karl. She looks nervous. Real nervous. "No, I haven't. It's since *we* got here. Not since Amanda got here."

I lean in, "What?"

She waves it off, "Never mind."

I nod and look for the waitress but I can't see her anywhere. There's too many scrawny gay guys and fat lesbians in the way, so I can't see a damn thing. After a couple minutes of this, I get up and slip through a sea of glittered midriff, body piercings and pungent odors. A stinking cocktail of dozens upon dozens of different perfumes, hair products and body sprays, the stench of sweat and body odor permeating everything.

On a night like this *Chambers* swells up beyond capacity so that every person is in your elbow space. Every single person is actively vacuuming up the oxygen around you, vaporizing it from the vicinity.

I wave at the bartender and shout out for three beers. He gives them to me but when I hand him a twenty the waitress, the blonde-leggy-model-thing, she snatches the money from him and pushes it back into my palm. There's so many people around I can't hear what she's saying and I can't tell if she's talking to me or the bartender, so I just pocket the twenty, raise the beers to her and nod appreciatively before slipping back into the crowd of colliding queers.

Sims

Back at the booth I put the booze on the table and sit down. Karl and Alison are gone, but I can see them mashing into each other on the dance floor, not noticing the dirty looks being shot at them by the surrounding dykes bopping up and down on the floor. I chug my beer and sip the one I brought for Alison.

In this light people look like faded versions of themselves. Pale skin flashing in and out of focus under a disco ball, cheap stimuli, revolving aimlessly in the center of the room. Everybody looking like a dull color photocopy of their actual self. Everyone swinging their bodies to the same beat, the same chorus, yet each vessel of flesh sways slightly out of synch with the next. In my opinion, the only kind of dancing that makes any sense is choreographed dancing, but anything choreographed is too premeditated, too rehearsed to be anything but unnatural. Martha Graham said that dance is the hidden language of the soul. Ruth St. Denis described dance as being used as communication between body and soul, to express what is too deep for words. Looking at the small mob of men and women flailing this way and that, knocking into and another, I see nothing inspired. I just see what is probably a thousand dollars' worth of booze swishing about inside the bellies of these serial one-night standers. Angela Monet once said that those who danced were thought to be quite insane by those who could not hear the music, I guess this is true in my case, because the more I watch these strangers straddling one another on a foggy floor, one that hides their feet entirely, I feel colder and colder inside my skin, I feel frozen at the bones, chilled in the guts. I feel alone, empty and apathetic.

"...ends in about ten minutes."

I look up; the waitress-model-blonde thing is standing in front of me waving her cell phone in front of her. "Mind if I join you after?"

The beer I'm holding is empty. I look from my hand to the vacant seats around me. Karl and Alison still bumping and grinding each other in the fog, under the disco ball.

The waitress touches my arm, winks and walks away, her body swallowed up by the crowd. I go to the restroom, stand around and watch she-males stroke layers and layers of mascara onto fake eyelashes until a stall opens up and I can take a piss. On the wall someone's written 'Sticks and stones may break my bones, but whips and chains excite me. So, throw me down, and tie me up and show me that you like me.' Underneath is a heart painted in orange nail polish. I push my thumb in the middle of it and when I take it away, my print fades away instantly from the cold white tile.

Outside the stall a girl is pounding on the door next to mine, talking to her friend who's bent over the sink and leaning right into the mirror. I can see them through the little space between my door and the wall. The girl pounding on the next door, she's saying, "Hurry up! I gotta go so bad I have to take a number four!" The chick inside on the toilet says, "What the hell is a number *four?*"

Pounder girl just keeps hammering on the stall, "I gotta *go!* Hurry up asshole!"

The girl on the toilet clicks her heels on the floor, I hear her farting a little. "Fuck off, bitch!"

Pounder slaps the door one more time, walks over to her friend at the mirror who says, "Where did you get that shirt?"

"I know! Nice, huh? I like it. It looks great right?"

"Yeah, but it would look better in the garbage."

I flush the toilet and don't bother washing my hands on the way out.

Alison and Karl are still dancing. I wave at them as I walk by, but they don't see me. I think about going to the bar and getting more beer, but I don't want to have to fight the crowd for one more stupid beer. So, I walk back to the booth. Some drunk guy is falling down close to some tables and reaching out for anybody to help brace him, he sees me, goes for a grab, I step out of the way and he topples over, his head slamming into the leg of a high stool. I think about maybe going for that beer again, but I see the waitress sitting at my table, her legs crossed. I'm too close to just walk away so I walk real slow up to her and slip into the booth, she reaches under the table and squeezes my knee.

"Amanda, right?"

"Hi."

"You remember me?"

I smile. "*You* remember *me*?"

She purrs like a kitten and slides over towards me putting an arm around my shoulder. "How could I forget these eyes?" A polished fingernail glides over my eyebrows. "And this hair. Goddamn, is it this dark naturally or do you dye?"

"I never dye. I'm naturally black."

"I see. How do you get it so straight?"

"I straighten it."

"With a hair straightener?"

Up close her tits look a lot bigger. She's got them pressed against me so close I can feel the rise and fall of her breath. She doesn't seem to care that I'm staring at them. She smiles when I smile because she thinks I'm thinking about sucking her milk makers. And she's half right. I may be looking at her jugs, but I'm also looking for an entry point. It's said that the human heart creates enough pressure while pumping to squirt blood thirty feet into the air. Looking at her heaving chest, I'm wondering if this is true.

"Uh huh."

She cocks an eyebrow, grinning as she leans in to kiss me.

She tastes like vodka and watermelons. Her hair smells like jasmine drowned in ammonia. She slips a finger between our lips giggling and nibbles at my earlobe. I think of Alison tearing at her nails, wiping her spit on my hand. I kiss her fingertip anyway. A lot of people think that after you die your hair and fingernails continue to grow. Although entertaining, this isn't true. What happens is the skin dehydrates and pulls away from the nails and hair. It looks like they're getting longer, but it's really the opposite. The body is shrinking.

She leans away, smiling, her eyes falling down to her lap, her teeth biting her lip. "You're so cute...in that way."

I kiss her. "Oh?"

"Huh?"

"In what way?"

She grins again, her eyes moving across my face, she's talking to my neck when she says, "That creepy way. Like, all dark and pale and..." She giggles. "...I've always had a thing for Wednesday Addams."

"Oh?" I'm sort of creeped out that she is comparing me to a fictional character and what's worse is that character is a child.

She kisses me hard. "I'm going to fuck the shit out of you tonight."

I brush the hair away from her face, slipping my hands loosely around her neck. If you kneel on somebody's chest, cover their nose and mouth, and push their jaw upwards you can induce fatal asphyxiation without any visible injuries.

I kiss her softly in the back of the taxi. "Is that so?"

She rubs a hand across my chest, cups one of my breasts and licks the side of my face. "Come. My place tonight. You can stay, but I need you gone by morning."

"Don't worry." I touch her chest, feel her heart beating. "You won't even hear me leave."

Chapter 6

My mother told me that when I was born, we laid in bed for those first three days. She said I spent the entire time with my eyes closed, my hands not leaving her hair. She took her baths sitting on the edge of the mattress, her feet in a washtub as Marcy ran a sponge down her back. We lay there on that dusty sunken pad of broken springs, my mother spooning the meals brought to her while I fed from her breasts, staring wide eyed into nothing. On the morning of the fourth day we rose because somewhere between the break of night and all its darkness and the blue beginnings of dawn, her warm breast slipped from my mouth and I cried for the first time. Ancient blankets bundled around me, I sneezed from all the dust buried in the wool. My mother said she picked me up, carried me to the window and pointed to the still fields surrounding that dead house. She told me she was looking at the stars as they faded out of the sky, saying my name to herself over and over as each one went back into the black of space and all its emptiness. She said she didn't care, because I was the only light needed, the rising sun come to chase away the darkness. She said she told me this, but when she took me off her shoulder and cradled me in her arms, I was asleep. And soon, so was she.

    I was crawling when the wrecking ball came. It shattered the living room with one swoop. Marcy was on the toilet, my mom chucking corn in the kitchen while I explored the shadows of empty cupboards. Depending on how drunk she was, the story always changed when she told it to me years later. Sometimes the ball was far from me, sometimes close, but how we left the place was always the same. We always ran out the back door, my mother and I squeezed together, chest to chest, Marcy behind, stiff strips of wheat whipping us raw as we tore through the fields. None of us had dry eyes when the construction workers chased us down. None of us had any shoes on when the sheriff put us in his car.

    When the former owners of the house came into the police station and saw mom and Marcy, heard me screaming in the social work room, they decided not to press charges. They gave mom two hundred dollars and the phone number of their church's minister. Mom took the money but she threw the seven digits in the trash after they left.

Chapter 7

"How's your boss, how's he doing these days?"

"Blaine? He's fine." I drop a dish in the soapy water, pull the plug and let it drain a little before turning the tap to hot and filling the sink back up.

Marcy pushes her wheelchair towards the miniature Christmas village, each tiny glass house lined up neatly beside the other on top of an old coffee table. "How's about the other fellas in your department? You got any boys you'd like to bring back to introduce me to?"

I turn off the tap. "In customer service? Naw Marcy, you wouldn't be interested in meeting any of the people I work with."

She touches a miniature church, pinching the cotton coming out of the chimney. "Oh, come on now. I wouldn't mind. I haven't seen you bring home a fellow in years. Just those friends of yours." She turns her wheelchair around. "Those *girls*...."

I drop a pot in the water, steam rising, burning into my eyes. "Isn't *As The World Turns* on?"

She looks at the cuckoo clock above her TV. "About ten minutes still."

I look back at her sitting there, breath in her chest, frowning and drumming her fingers on the gray rubber of the chair's wheels. "You wouldn't want to meet any of the guys I work with."

"Huh?" She looks at the linoleum. "Why? They a horny bunch or something?"

I sigh, drop a handful of forks and knives in the sink, water splashing the stomach of my t shirt, "All boys are, aren't they?"

She sounds nervous when she laughs, her voice fading to mumbles mid-sentence. "That's what your mother always used to say about that..."

"Well," I drop another handful of silverware in the sink, that sound of steel scraping hard against partially submerged dishes. "She was right, I guess."

Marcy wheels over to the couch, picks up the remote control, looks at the clock and wheels back to where I'm standing. "I'd like to see you with someone. I'd like to be around for a wedding."

She frowns, looks down at her slippered feet. "You know that."

Chunks of old spaghetti sauce float to the top of the water. They look like flakes of dried blood. I run more hot water, squeezing the bottle of dish soap into the stream. "Marcy, it's just not... I'm not *ready*, you know? Some people aren't maybe meant for lov—meant for marriage. I'm one of those people, I'm..."

"Amanda Troy! You look at me right now!"

I bow my head and turn off the tap.

"Amanda Francis, *look* at me right now!"

I look at her. Her little fists knotted like bony balls of meaty yarn, her blonde hair going gray at the roots. She has the same eyes as my mom; the same eyes as me. We have almost the exact same mouth, except I have three scars on my chin, and one long one beside my mouth. These are claw marks from the first girl that I raped and murdered. She kept screaming through the whole thing, but the real problem was: I don't have a penis. If I had a penis, things would have been a lot simpler. I could've fucked her, pulled out and ran when I finished. But if I let her go, police would have known to be on the lookout for a woman and it wouldn't take long before my description was sketched on every newspaper. Besides, being a woman, raping other women, they put up more of a fight. Chicks will lay there while a dude drives hard, banging away balls deep in her. Half the time girls don't say anything because they don't want to get popped in the head by a guy who's three times stronger than they are. They don't want to risk a shattered nose, broken jaw, even then, laying spread eagle in the bushes, spirits shattering with every thrust, their vanity is still telling them not to piss him off because they could wind up with a bald patch, or a bruise, or a broken jaw. But in reality, there is nothing more violent and torturous than lesbian rape. Because most women don't get off as simply as men and you're working with a different set of genitals than guys, so there's a lot of other things you have to use to compensate. Anyway, afterwards I choked her to death and then broke her neck. I was so scared I'd get caught, but blood was coming out of my face like a faucet so I had no choice but to go to the emergency room. When they glued the cuts together, when the nurses all gathered around me stroking my hair and telling me it was going to be alright, that I was beautiful and they were so sorry, I had the same look in my eyes as Marcy does right now.

"Don't you *ever* say that! Your mother would say that! I'd hear her say that over and over again. Every day the same thing, the same 'I don't deserve love' garbage!"

In the emergency room, I told them I was raped. When I showed up in triage with five deep slashes on the back of my shoulder, fingernail gashes splitting my face open, they got Victims Assistance to pay for a new outfit. A week later the cops called me up and I got twenty-five hundred dollars from Crime Stoppers for pointing out the right guy in a police lineup. Turns out the guy really was a rapist, and after I randomly fingered him, he admitted to the cops everything he'd done to some woman in the park. The women of this city really should be thanking me.

"You're *beautiful*! Amanda, you are a beautiful person, inside and out. Don't you go second guessing that, second guessing yourself around *me*!"

I scratch my neck, hot water dripping down the collar of my t-shirt absorbing into my bra. "Thank you, Marcy."

She holds her glare at me for a moment, then wheels back over to the couch and turns on the TV. The volume is nearly deafening and I have to strain to hear her say, "Give me strength Francis."

I lean back over the sink and slap a dish towel over my shoulder. "Shouldn't you be asking God?"

She looks at me like I've said 'fuck' in church. "Now why would I do a crazy thing like that?"

Chapter 8

If we let them use the bathroom, customers would come in the bathroom non-stop. No pun intended. They would *literally* coat the entire room with jizz. Take for instance this guy, he's been in the store for a solid four hours, asking to use the bathroom every twenty minutes. A replica Great Dane penis toy the size of a thermos and a pig tail butt plug are tucked under each arm, he slips his middle finger in and out of the silicone Audrey Hollander ass /pussy, on the shelf. And every twenty minutes he moves down a model, poking a wiggly finger in and out of the little plastic circle cut out of every box. Then asks to use the bathroom.

I say no and he returns to finger banging Nikki Benz, digging around inside Ginger Lynn's asshole, tickling Mary Carey's rubber clit, he skips Jada Fire and moves on to pinch Silvia Saint's swollen cunt lips. ll the while coughing into his fist. I'd ask him to stop or please leave, but he's bringing items to the till, dropping them on the table and running back to the shelves. This guy comes in every couple weeks, looking like he hasn't slept. He comes in here looking like he hasn't eaten anything except hooker pussy. It's true, every time he wanders in here, he looks thinner and thinner. I don't know his name, and I don't think I want to. All I know is comes in here, drops a few hundred dollars on porn and takes Lilly back to his motel room when he can afford it. It only sucks because Lilly, one of the many prostitutes that hangs around the side of the store at night, is the only girl I actually sort of like. It's kind of depressing when I think about it; depressing in the sense that an eighteen-year-old runaway turned prostitute, who does way too much coke and smokes like a Nazi *and* is the only person I am capable of having partial feelings for. Yeah, it's sort of depressing when I think about it, so mostly I try not to. I just close my eyes and ride the waves of euphoria whenever she's down there, kissing and sucking on whatever I've got my pants pulled down past.

"How much for that?" The skinny guy, the silicone finger banger points behind me. I grab a vinyl blindfold off the wall.

"Sixteen bucks."

He nods, gets his wallet out from the back of his sagging jeans. "Kay, I'll take two of those."

I pull another one down, ring in his total.

He squints, coughs into his fist and puts down his credit card. His eyes are so bloodshot they look like they could pop at any minute.

When he leaves, Blaine comes out of his office, stumbling toward me, eyes on a clipboard he's got firm in his hands. "Amanda, did we sell out of those gag balls already?" He scratches his head and hands the clipboard to me. "Says we have three in stock still, but..." He turns to where the gags are shelved. "...I can't find them any place."

"Hmm, yeah I remember selling some last week but..." I study the inventory. According to this list we have a serious shortage of blow up dolls and BDSM bed restraints.

He takes the clipboard back. "Probably stolen. Keep a closer eye out here, I guess." He scratches his head, rubs a hand down the shirt buttons of his gut and looks at his watch. "Break time, get out of here. See you in twenty."

I grab my coat from under the till and feel the pockets for my cigarettes on my way out the back. I light one as I lean against the building, blowing blue smoke out of my lungs as I look up at where the stars are supposed to be. Inner city like this, it's almost impossible to see anything through the unending luminescence and pollution amassing overhead. Almost impossible to see anything beautiful and glowing above you, burning from millions of miles away. In this city, you look up and see only patrolling helicopters circling with their spotlights switched on, or the wings of airplanes blinking red as they take off, as they come in. It makes me glad to know I live far enough away from the city that I can still gaze up at the night sky and see the beauty of midnight. It makes me glad to know I live far enough way, but close enough to hurt it.

"Well hello there, stranger!" Lilly appears from the side of the building, the fingertips of an outstretched hand drag lightly along the brick as she walks towards me in red heels.

"Hiya, Lil." I get out a cigarette and hand it to her.

"Why thank you, love. How's work?" She leans against the building, close enough that our shoulders touch. Her tiny leather jacket presses soundlessly against my cotton zipper sweater.

"It goes. You?"

She says "Ha, ha, ha" pausing between each 'ha' for a full second.

"Sucks *dick*." This time she really does laugh, but only for pretend.

I hand her my lighter. "Didn't go home with what's his face?"

The flame lighting up her face, she's stunning. Gorgeous in that wasted junkie way most nihilistic German artists or depressed euro trash models look. Only she's got blonde hair instead of black and skin so flawless you have to stare hard to see that the dark under her eyes isn't from smudged makeup, but from lack of sleep. She shakes her head, "No, he tried taking me back. But I told him I'm not going there for any less than sixty-five."

"Oh."

"Yeah, so instead he gave me thirty."

"For what?"

She shrugs, taps the ash off her smoke. "Quick hand and a blow."

"Cool."

"Not really. That fuckers into some weird shit. I don't know if I would go back with him even if he did have the cash." She takes a drag. "Well, for eighty maybe, hundred for sure."

"Yeah, guy seems a little weird."

"Why? He ever try picking you up?" I can feel her tense up beside me, but she relaxes when I tell her no. He's never tried paying me for sex.

"Good." She taps the ash off again. "Weird shit I tell you. That fuckers into some weird shit."

"Like how?"

"Well, I don't know. In my line of work, you see it all the time. These guys are so addicted to sucking and fucking, it's like each time you see them it gets worse and worse. Six months into one regular and he'll be parked in an alley while you blow guys. Just parked there watching you, waiting for you to finish sucking stranger's dicks so you can go over to him and squeeze the cum out of the rubbers you used all over his face. And he'll just sit there for like two hours, sitting in his car and not wiping the cum off his face. So, every time you empty a rubber on his face it just gets messier and messier, all that goop dripping in his eyes, pooling in the corners of his mouth. He's inhaling semen up his goddamn *nostrils*."

"Who? This guy?" I hike a thumb over my shoulder at the store. "The guy who was just in here does that?"

"No, no. Not him. Another guy."

"Oh, okay."

"No, what that guy who was just in there is into is worse. Well, not really *worse* worse, but definitely weirder."

"How do you figure?"

She laughs, taps the ash and takes a drag. "Well, like I said, I definitely wouldn't go back to his place for anything less than a hundred now. Not after last time."

I laugh. "Lil, are you gonna tell me or what?"

"Yeah...." She waves some smoke away from her face. "Shit, that just got in my eye."

"Yeah, I hate when that happens."

"It *hurts*, goddamn!" She bends over for a second, her hand to her face, then leans back against the wall, her leather jacket reflecting dull shades from the building's security lights.

"What's his name?"

She rubs her eye with the knuckle of her finger. "Rick."

"Oh. Gross."

She laughs, slaps my arm. "I *know*, right?"

"Anyways, this guy Rick, *last* time he picks me up, yeah? And he takes me back to this real seedy motel. Like roaches in the tub sort of seedy, ya know?"

"Uh huh."

"Well, we're in the room and he's like 'One sec.' So, I sit on the bed and wait for him to come back and when he does, he's carrying this birdcage, with a towel over it. He puts it down, right, he takes the towel off and the second he does this damn bird starts tweeting like a crazy thing. So like, I'm sitting there wondering '*what the hell he wants me to do with this damn bird?*' I'm thinking, there's no way I'm putting that *fucking bird in my pussy* or some shit. And he's just standing there, right, not doing anything!"

She brushes some hair out of her face and licks her beautiful lips. "...and I start to get scared that like maybe he's going to bite the fuckin' things head off! Ozzy Osborne style, ya know? I start to get scared maybe he's some sort of animal torturing Satanist motherfucker and he's going to sacrifice me right there on that ugly fuckin' bed in that dirty fuckin' room."

She takes a drag of her cigarette, butts it out and flicks it out into the alley. "Anyway, after a couple real slow minutes he opens the cage, and I'm ready to bolt at this point because I'm so freaked out at what he might do."

"Yeah, I can imagine."

"I know, right? Then he opens the cage and grabs the bird..."

"What kind of bird?"

"Oh, I don't know. No wait, yeah, it was a pigeon."

"A pigeon?"

"Yeah, a goddamn pigeon! He takes out the pigeon and hands it to me. I'm like '*what the fuck?*' but I don't say anything because this guy pays good money. And I've got this fucking diseased animal in my hands. And I have no idea what's going on or how the fuck I'm gonna get him off with this ugly thing..."

"Rats of the sky."

"Huh?"

"Pigeons. They're the rats of the sky."

She laughs, smiling so big I can see all her teeth. "I *know*, I know!"

"So, what? Did he make you eat it? Hold it while he fucked you?"

She waves her hand, tosses back some hair and gestures to me for another cigarette. I light it in my mouth and pass it to her.

"No. Worse." She takes a puff and then spits on the ground. She exhales while she's talking, "He got down on his knees, put his hands behind his back and said 'I want you to swing it in circles. Just swing it in circles by the feet so the wings can touch my cock, but only at the end, before I come. I don't want to feel the feathers on my cock until I'm about to come. I just want to feel the wind first.' So, I hold its feet and start swinging the thing around and around in circles. The whole time he's got his eyes shut, just moaning and moaning. I go faster and faster, the bird flapping its wings, not making a fuckin' sound. I felt kinda bad, but I just wanted to get it over with, so I kept doing it."

She takes a deep drag off the cigarette and pulls a strand of blonde hair out of the corner of her mouth. "Finally, he shouts '*I'm coming! I'm coming!*' The wings barely graze his dick and he shoots all over the rug, I'm talking projectile orgasm release. This weird fucker, he blows on the rug and even gets a little on my boots, which I didn't really care about because I don't really like those boots anyway. But he gets it on them just the same. After that..." She takes an anxious drag, the orange cherry on the end of her smoke glowing bright before ash covers it. "Well, after that he just pulls up his pants, tosses some twenties on the bed and leaves. He *leaves* me in his own goddamn room still holding this dizzy fuckin' bird. So that's why I don't think I'll go back with him anymore. Not for less than a hundred anyway."

I light a smoke, roll a pebble under my sneaker. "So, what happened to the bird?"

"Oh. I just put him out on the deck as I was leaving. I watched him trip around for a couple seconds. Then he flew off."

I laugh. She pinches my arm. "Ow! Lil!"

"Poor thing. I wonder what was going through its mind as it flew around the city. I mean, if pigeons *can* talk to each other like we do, I wonder what *that* one would say, and how the hell the other ones peeking around in the park for bread crumbs and French fries, how *they* would interpret the story."

I pinch her arm back. "No idea."

She's quiet for a minute. I check my watch; my shift starts again in five minutes. "Well, I gotta go back in. Pay the bills. You know."

She smiles, leans in and kisses me. "And what about *my* bills, Amanda?"

I feel her waist, her tight stomach. I think of her pussy when I kiss her and I think of the dead girl still in my basement and why I can't bring Lilly back home with me tonight. "You're richer than I am." I pinch her nose. "Quit blowing it all up here."

She laughs, "You wanna line? A line before you head back to work?"

"Naw, I'm good. Thanks."

"Oh, come on!"

She pounds her little fist against my heart. "*One!*"

"Yeah, okay fine." I take her to my car, snort a line and eat her out. Her pussy tastes like condoms but I don't care. Before I go back in the store I try and give her thirty bucks but she won't take it. "Save it. Buy some groceries and make me dinner sometime."

I pinch her ass and walk back in fifteen minutes late. Blaine is in his office and there's no one in the store. I sit there at the till watching cars go by, looking for any that turn in to the side to pick Lilly up. I think about spaghetti, big fat meatballs; I wonder if Marcy has a recipe book for Italian food upstairs. I think about that red dress I bought last autumn and my cute black Mary Jane flats; I think about wearing them for Lilly. I think of all these things until I see a car turn into the alley beside the store. A minute later I see the car pulling out onto the highway in front, I see Lilly looking in her purse and the person behind the wheel is just a figure, cloaked in shadow.

I try and think about what drink would go good with pasta. I think about wine selections—but then the wine turns to blood. The spaghetti becomes intestines, and the meat balls—just wads of rolled human muscle tooth-picked together and burnt to a crisp. I'm not wearing my red dress anymore, I'm covered in the dark gush of approximately five to six litres of blood. Whoever's blood it is, I don't care, it doesn't matter. Because we're all so goddamn evil, that none of us deserve to live.

Chapter 9

"Attention customers, this week's discount is on all product price tags marked red. Do you have a special someone in your life that you would like to show a little extra love? Well then, be sure to browse our wide selection of various discount items in the women's section. This includes beauty, kids..." The buzzing voice of the female announcer coughs loud into the microphone. "...makeup....no wait. All these wonderful products marked down to affordable price...marked *as* affordable and made even *more* afford...cheaper than before! Prices going way down! As low as ninety percent on some brand name...."

I pick up a bag of chips and stare at the cheetah standing on its hind legs. He is wearing sun shades and grinning a mouth full of perfect teeth. I heard on TV once that lions hunting gazelle will always go for the sickly one. The lionesses will run down the slowest weakest gazelle and then chew its back until it drops. Even before its dead, the sick gazelle is devoured by a group of giant starving kitty cats.

The announcer coughs again, she coughs *loudly*. Distortion cracks through the speakers, popping our ears, making us grind our teeth with the buzz shock scrambling through our ear canals. "Mothers will be glad to hear that children's grape flavored liquid Tylenol is now thirty percent off as well as *all* No Name chewable vitamins D, C and..." Another loud cough, I almost bite my tongue.

    I want to live in the rain forest. And never die. I want to live behind a waterfall and mouth feed snakes on the grass. Somewhere in the distance, a Toucan calls and a monkey answers.

    The bag of chips crunches in my hand, I try and puff it back up to look normal again but, I'm stuck looking at the grinning cheetah with its black glasses and petite physique. All the bright orange food sealed inside a plastic bag. Between another loud cough over the PA and my left ear pops. The thought hits me that maybe this is how they get us—the lions I mean. They feed us this orange shit so we can't move fast enough to get away, or we consume so much that this crap actually starts gnawing away at our brains, children with developing cognitive skills are slowed down by the high doses of preservatives and cheese coloring until they are too stupid to realize that the very real danger of death is upon them. I look down the aisle at a woman with an ass so big she could be smuggling a locker room's worth of basketballs in her shorts. I put the bag back and wipe my hand on my shirt. Call me crazy, but I'd rather be a cannibal than a fat person.

    I leave the isle but don't grab much. Just some apples, some oranges, a loaf of bread. Even though I know where they put it, I ask a cute girl with a price gun where the hair dye is. I drop a box of black into my shopping basket and wait in line. Whether you choose to or not, in America you *have* to follow the lives of celebrities. Whether it interests you or not, you still know the basics of who's who, who's marrying so and so, and when what's-her-face is apologizing for getting caught drinking and driving again. You know this because you buy bread. Or you buy dish soap or discounted jeans and you pay for them at the till and at the till is a long

Sinners Circle

rack of celebrity magazines with carefully placed much needed items you may or may not have forgotten to buy while browsing. Items like shaving razors, double A batteries, tooth brushes and breath mints. These items are of course the most expensive brand names on the market, this is why they put them here. Impulse spending is the staple of our economy; when you buy an eight-dollar triple blade razor because you don't have the time to run back to the aisle where they sell them in bulk for half the price. But you might not remember, because you've been stuffing your brains full of that orange food. So now, the lions are going to get you.

But, you're not just adding an extra line of black ink to your receipt, when purchasing impulse items. With every stick of junk you throw in your cart at the last second, that you applying the glue to the economy. Besides, who'd want to run back and grab a shaving razor when you just find out what's-his-nuts parading on the cover of People magazine as the World's Sexiest Man Alive. But it's not enough to know who won, but who *could* have won. Now you can argue with your friends about it.

As much as you may like it, or dislike it, it's a fact. Your involvement with the rich and famous is no longer a choice, even if you hide in your house all day reading the bible and loading your guns, sooner or later you are going to have to buy toilet paper when the phone book runs out of pages. So, you will have to come here, and you will have to look at every one of these magazines with yellow letters that burn into your brain before you can stop yourself from reading "DIVORCED" or "BACK TO REHAB."

However, today is lucky. Today, the ladies in line aren't pawing over glossy covers with smirking models they could never look like. No, today the ladies in line are burying their faces inside a newspaper, mouths ringed like they're sucking a Cheerio. In between swiping items across the counter even the cashier is glancing at a copy lying open beside her. Everyone's got the paper folded and askew so I can't really see what's on the front. The rack where they keep the local newspaper is empty. I stand on my tippy toes for a second, look around then back at the empty tray. I notice there's a copy crammed at the bottom with the *Wall Street Journal*. I pick it up and flip it over to the front.

"*Model/Waitress Found Slashed In Apartment.*" There's a big color picture of her in her high school graduation robes, blonde, pretty and smiling. Midway through the article are enlarged letters in italic quotation marks "*...tied to a chair, arms and legs bound, saran wrap still clinging to her bludgeoned skull. Police estimate she was found three days after time of death. The body was found by a visiting relative, Tuesday. Family beside itself with grief.*"

Flipping to the second page, scrolling for some quotations, I read, "We do not understand how this could have happened to someone like our Kimberly. She was friendly, outgoing, kind and warm hearted to all those around her. She and her fiancé had lost a baby to miscarriage last year and it was hard for her dealing with that, but she was getting better, *doing* better. Kim's modeling career had really started to take off, she was going to get married next month in Florida.... our hearts are broken. But we know she is with God now and this is in His hands. I can't imagine why any man would want to do this to our poor little Kimberly."

Beside the article is a sketch of a man police gathered descriptions of from witnesses in the building around the time of Kim's death. He looks like a fat Mexican traced in pencil.

"Is that everything?"

I look up from the newspaper. "Oh. Yeah, that's all of it. Thanks." I give my best smile.

"Psycho."

My heart skips a full two beats. "What?"

The cashier, she points at the newspaper in my hands, "In there. What a psycho, huh?"

I look at the paper, back at her. "Well, whoever it is, they've sure got some serious hang-ups with women."

Chapter 10

It was Thursday evening, and I was driving home. The sun was melting into the horizon, I roll up the windows, turn off the radio and start humming *House of the Rising Sun*. I watch the wheels of vehicles in front of me, my teeth vibrating, buzzing electric at my command.

I had a long day and dreaded being stuck in traffic, I didn't want to have to wait twenty, twenty-five minutes before I could get home and unwind. I touched my clit, giving it little taps to the rhythm of *The House of the Rising Sun*, while my teeth buzzed, my mouth motionless while I hummed.

I felt hot, long stabs of rage shock through my chest, brain and hands. I shouted the rest of the song, angry, punching the wheel and dashboard every few words... 'mother'... 'tell your children'.... 'wear that ball and chain...'

I swerved to the shoulder of the road and pulled over. I almost did a little drift and I hoped someone saw it and thought it looked cool. I never get to look cool. Thinking of that reminded me a Neil Young song, *Keep on Rock'n in the Free World* and how bad abortion is because it's like, that kid, will never get to be cool. Because his moms a bitch.

I got out of the car, humming to myself as I walked over to the side of the road and looked into the dark woods. I was scared what was in there. I was scared that I'd find what I want. What I was looking for.

I started walking until I hit a thin path, curving behind some bushes. It gave me easy access inside the trees. I closed my eyes, cold winds bit into my nose and cheeks, as I stood, singing softly, '...keep on rock'n in the freee wooorld...."

Suddenly I felt my foot kick against something, I looked down at my sneaker. What looked like it was once a skunk or possibly a raccoon, was now a writhing mound of maggots and teeny, tiny worms. I stood there staring. I was entranced by the movement, that shook the pile, moving it this way and that like some unseen, uncontrollable force. And it reeked like death and decay. I covered my nose, took off my jacket and wrapped the dirty little thing up and carried it back to my car. I opened the truck, tossed the jacket into the trunk and slammed the lid. Then I got back in my car, turned on the radio and pulled back onto the highway.

The sun had gone down by the time I started driving home again., *Third Eye Blind* had come on the radio and I was in better spirits, tapping the wheel and singing *Semi-Charmed Life*.

I stuck to the back roads because there aren't any lights here. Just stop signs a mile away from the nearest house. I've always wanted to hit somebody with my car. I could pretend to stop at a crosswalk and then they would cross and then I could run them over and drive away and because nobody is around. I could completely get away with murder around here.

I laughed and rubbed my clit again. I could feel my cunt getting spiky. Like a bomb of tiny needles, exploding deep inside me like sunlight and it's like my actions, while this is happening, are the explosion damages of that bomb. So, it's not really my fault. It's God's problem. I turn off the radio and laugh, "Yeah, file the insurance claims under *Act of God* you fucking retards!"

I laugh again and turn the wheel into my drive way. I'm smiling when I get out.

A young girl walking to the park behind my house, catches my eye and smiles back, "Hi!"

"Hi, Karen!" I walk to the back of my car and open the trunk.

She stops walking and laughs. "What?"

I reach in and take my jacket with the mound of maggots. I'm closing the trunk and turning to the girl. "Oh, sorry, you look just like her. Are you heading to the park?"

Before she could answer, I sigh. "I found her little kitten on the highway just down there. "I pointed behind her. She turned then I stepped closer to her, her head snapped back when she noticed me advancing. I held up the jacket. "I think it's dead."

Her face fell, then it only took a second for me to catch a twinkle in her eye. A Black Star rises. She stepped closer. "Oh my God... can I see?"

I frowned and pretended to be really sad. "Well, okay. I have to wash him right now, or he might get an infection."

She followed me into my house.

When we stepped inside, she pretended not to be nervous. I said,

"Oh, could you take off your shoes please? I just got new carpeting."

She nodded, nervously bending forward to get at her shoes.

When she was halfway down I said, "Oh, here hold this for a sec."

I quickly handed her the jacket and as her hands stuck out to grab it, she was also rising to stand, which meant her footing was unbalanced. But only for that split second. I slapped my hand around her skull, my fingers full of her hair, I slammed the side of her skull into the peephole cover. She went down immediately. The jacket falling open, a spray of maggots tumbled out on top of her.

I stood there for a moment, admiring how beautiful she was and ball parking her age. I pegged her around twenty, *maybe* 22 because she's active enough to be going to a park, and exercise is attributed to maintaining youth.

I bent over her, leaning against the door, feeling bored. Imagining that I'm a teenager and I'm suffering of boredom in my room when all the sudden my amazing dad bursts through the door and says, "HEY! WE'RE GONNA DO SOMETHING EXCITING!"

I smiled down at her and brushed some hair out of her face with my shoe. "And that's gonna be you!"

I smiled, pretending it was Disneyland on Christmas. I walked around to her feet and dragged her into the living room. I sighed, I smiled. I rubbed my cunt and I jumped up and down. I walked back to the door and scooped up all the maggots I could. Kissing them in my hand. "Babies, momma's babies. Come love momma with me, babies."

I made my way back to her this way. Following a trail of maggots and kissing them every time my cunt throbbed. Every now and then I would laugh because I knew this was so crazy. But I didn't care. I was mainlining into ecstasy. I was alone with the God's, drowning deep in Hali.

When I was back at her side, she started to stir. She looked beautiful. I kicked her once, hard across the temple, and she was back out into Black Out. I envied her for that.

I sighed, looked down at her and whistled. Then I dragged her into my bedroom, threw her on the bed and looked in her wallet-purse thing. When I rob people, I like to play a game where, I don't get to look at the money part until I check the ID. If I have guessed right about their age, I get to see how much I've won. I know it doesn't matter really because, I'll always take the money anyway but, these are the games I get to play when I am in Disneyland on Christmas.

Her out of state Student ID tells me she is 22. I laugh, victorious at her, "Bitch!"

Then I use some light chain, coated in rubber tubing and cuff her legs open. Each leg apart, attached to the wall hook behind her. This way her cunt is upwards, twenty-four-seven. I cuff her wrists and attach them to a chain that runs to the foot of the bed and attaches to the bed frame, that I'd bolted to the floor during Shark Week. I mean on TV, not when I was having my period. It really bothers me when people jump to those stupid, sexist assumptions whenever you act irritated by them.

I kick the dresser and walk into the bathroom. I turn on the light and stare at my own reflection. It drives me nuts when somebody is being held accountable for bothering you, and you tell them to go away, that they don't accept *any* responsibility whatsoever.

I punch the mirror, slam the door and scream. I turn on the shower for extra noise cover. I shout "Nope! Not gonna learn. Never gonna fuck'n learn!"

I turn off the shower, swing open the door and march back into the bedroom. I move towards the bed and pull on her chains, testing their security.

I look down at her. She's breathing. Watching her sweet, wet little mouth. Her tiny tongue, so soft and unaware, happy to just be where it is. In its natural environment. At home and safe.

I felt my nipples get hard, I felt waves of euphoria wash through me. I felt dizzy and had to piss. I scooped up some maggots, gagging uncontrollably from the smell which stung my eyes, coating the back of my throat with a lining of vomit. I took off my pants and climbed onto the bed. I squatted above her, so we were pussy to pussy, and then I started to piss. I moaned, sprinkling maggots between her and I. Letting them arrive to mommy in a bath. Like little prince and princesses, in a surreal world, where all you have to do to be happy is eat and everyone loves each other. The smell of decay was so putrid, so vile that as I bounced the last bead of piss off my pussy, I vomited. Then a few seconds later I came.

But, I felt bad all of the sudden. Not so much ashamed but, sorry to have done this to her. To have polluted her with my filth. I watched her closely. She had very nice skin, and dark hair, like me but her hair was slightly longer than mine. But only by an inch.

I stood up, hopped off the bed and grabbed a towel. I ran the tap, watching the fabric melt into a dark, heavy cloth that felt warm in my hand. I hated how affectionate warm water was. I turned off the tap and walked back to the girl. I stood between her legs and washed off all the piss and carefully picked up all the maggots, and tossed them onto the bed, but further away from her.

I watched her stir again and was worried she'd start to scream. That would ruin everything and I started to seriously wonder if she would. I went into the kitchen and looked in my medicine cabinet. I always, *always* have some Xanax and Ativan on hand. I crushed up three bars and four tablets and stirred them into some warm water. This time, I was careful not to get any on my hands.

I waited a minute for the bars to completely dissolve, then I carried the glass into the bedroom and tilted her head into a gentle swallowing position. Then I closed her nose with two fingers and slowly poured the liquid in until she started choking. I stopped, waited for her to stop coughing, swallow a few times, then go back to panting. Then I poured more in. I did this until the glass was empty. Then I threw it in a corner, my eyes on her as her eyes blinked open at the sound of shattering glass. She looked frightened, which really disappointed me. Then I remembered the Black Star in her eye earlier and my sympathy dried up.

I walked around to the side of the bed where I had tossed all the maggots. I scooped up a handful and walked to the foot of the bed, smack between her legs. Her eyes rolled over to me.

I looked dead at her. "Do maggots gross you?" Then I slapped the handful of tiny Princes and Princesses that were now screaming and filthy, furious and scandalized.

I squished every single one of them into the slimy lips of her cunt. I gagged as the stench hit my nostrils like a lemon soaked in snot, left to bake in the desert sun. I picked up the roadkill and turned it over in my hands, trying to find the dirtiest, grossest part. I did. Among a cluster of torn flesh, turned to open sores oozed congealed blood, crushed organs filled with maggots, bones laced with worms. I put my hand inside the creature and took hold of a wriggling ball of rot. It reeked so bad I barfed, but only a little. The odor alone gave me goosebumps. Actual chills ran down my spine, which sent waves of electricity up into my cunt, which roared in ecstasy every time the sour stench cut into my nostrils.

I rubbed it first against my own cunt. I closed my eyes and pushed a wad of tiny wriggling royalty, deep inside my own filthy cunt. I fell against the wall, squirming in orgasms that spasmed through me with a feeling so powerful, it could explain why people in Africa think demon possession is real. Because they're dirty and they stink and their pussies are full of maggots. That's why the women are acting so dumb. I shrieked with laughter as a glorious, God sent bob of my little babies began wiggling their fat little bodies all around my G-spot.

I went to stand but I kept cumming, I squeezed my legs together, trapping all the little babies inside of me. I fell forward and gripped the bed. My legs were shaking over a pool of wet, dripping out from between my legs. I realized there was going to be some screaming, so I slowly waddled over to the radio by my bed.

Third Eye Blind, was playing again and I sang loud between orgasms.

I took another heaping handful of maggots. They smelled so bad I gagged. Sharp as a bath of lava, they were literally falling out of this dead thing now. Still, no matter how many times I do this, I'm always surprised how many there are.

Semi-Charmed Life is kicking into chorus and I was singing along, but it really hit me that, what song I *really* like from Third Eye Blind is, *Jumper*. I dunno, I really like that song. I think the lyrics are beautiful and they got the chords right. *Jumper* is a far better song than *Semi-Charmed Life* in my opinion. Although *Semi-Charmed is* catchy. And it helped me twice today with getting into a better mood. Still, I think it's because *Semi-Charmed Life* is about friends and love and I don't have that so I can't really relate to it in the way I can relate to *Jumper* because *Jumper* is about wanting to die and overcoming pain. And I can relate to that. So, I like *Jumper* more but *Semi-Charmed Life* is not without its charm either. Ya' know?

I spat on her maggot smashed cunt lips then crammed my maggoty fist down, deep inside her cunt. Then another. Then another. I stuffed and stuffed until I had to hold my hands over the heaping mound of maggots, slithering in and out, tunneling, chewing, polluting her with filth so vile, so deep that it chewed on her bones.

I closed my eyes and tuned out the radio. I started to buzz my teeth together. I started humming *House of the Rising Sun* again. I walked over to the radio and turned it off, singing at the top of my lungs… 'I'm gooooing back to New Orleans to wear….. that ball and chaaain…..'

"What… are you… doing?

She was looking at me. Her eyes wide as quarters. She looked afraid. I felt embarrassed. I was silent, trying to think of something to say. As I waited, I smeared some maggot guts and animal rot across my chest. I deserved it. It reeked. My nose and eyes stung in sour agony. It was only fair. I didn't want her feeling like I was better than her. I did not want her to think that I was a monster. But as just a dirty, filthy human being. So she didn't have to feel afraid that I was a some monster going to gobble her up. Her eyes were wide, her face was set in that mode of terror that goes so deep, and is so gripping that the person actually appears calm. This is the first stage of shock. The biggest *pro* in this category is, I have her complete and total attention and interest. I felt my heart wash over with love for her.

I step closer, my maggoty hands stretching out to her. I smiled. "I'm sorr..."

For all the drugs she was on, she sure screamed loud. I couldn't believe it.

I put a pillow over her face. I wasn't going to suffocate her, I just needed a moment to think. I looked around the room as, my thoughts began darting. I didn't want to make a mess, chopping her up alive. Also, she will scream if I cram anything else inside her and I still want to put more inside her and if she screams it will distract me. What I really want to do is cuddle her while she is warm, then in the morning when she is cold I can chop her to bits and take really nice, clean shot photographs without all the blood in the way. People are always taking pictures of bloody this and bloody that and after a while it gets dull because I want to see the close-up decomposition process without all the color fucked up from all the fucking blood everywhere. Fuck.

She was thrashing beneath me. Her fingernails tearing into my belly. I loved it. I let up on the pillow a little bit to keep her fighting then I leaned in heavy against her windpipe. I closed my eyes and imagined the maggots inside my cunt where eating their way through me. That I was being eaten alive. I was *alive*.

As her clawing got weaker, I leaned in even harder, then I gave her a little air, then felt the burst of her nails, tearing into me. I thought how Ying and Yang this situation was right now. I closed my eyes again, this time with a peacefulness. I thought how it would feel being eaten alive, then I laughed because *she* will be dead and will be eaten by maggots. And if she was alive while that was happening, she would be feeling exactly what I was feeling that this exact moment, as she digs into me.

Even though, she'd gone limp, I started wondering if Stephan Jenkins was secretly a homo. I laid there for a really long time thinking about how gay he looked in all their music videos I'd seen on MTV. I really missed, Kurt Cobain.

After a while I sat up. I lifted the pillow and pinch her warm little cheeks. When girls die, and they're drugged, their corpses never look as terrifying. For instance, this girl here looks like she's fast asleep… covered in maggots. I lean in and kiss her forehead while closing her eyes. Then I walked to the foot of the bed, buzzing my teeth and humming quietly. 'I waaant something eeeelse….'

Chapter 11

Before I go to work, I deal with the body of the girl in my bed. But first I shower again. After last night, I scrubbed myself out and all over. This morning I did it again. Then I dragged the body to the basement door, opened it, pushed the body down. I head back to the bed room but stop when I see the axe I was going to look for was in the living room, against the couch. I pick it up, turn on the light above the basement stairs and close the door behind me. I toss the axe down as well because, I didn't want to fall and have an accident because I was holding an axe. I posed the body, like she was laying down, her legs spread open, totally willing.

    I push more maggots inside her and use my foot to stomp them in. I swing the axe, severing the tendons in her thighs, so her legs open wider. Then I sink the axe into the floor beside the body and run upstairs. I turn off the basement light and jump in the shower.

    There's slugs in the drain I think. I read somewhere that when your water backs up in the shower sometimes, slugs in the pipes is a possibility. I think it happens a lot in England. Something to do with the rainy weather. I towel off then throw on some jeans and a t-shirt. I look at my shoes and walk over to the closet. There's a mound of identical cheap sneakers I picked up at K-Mart last year. I put some new ones on and carry the old one out with me to the car. I swing by a corner store, toss the shoes in the trash and pick up a pack of cigarettes.

    Alison is outside, shaking out a floor mat. She waves at me as I pull into a parking space in front of where I work. She works at a coffee shop to doors from me here. I put the car into park and wave back.

    It's still ten minutes too early for my shift to start so I follow Alison inside the shop. I don't drink a lot of coffee so, maybe this will be like a treat for me. She's wiping down tables when I come in and she tosses the rag onto an empty chair, wraps her bracelets, and arms around me and gives me a hug.

    "Hi hun, how are you this lovely morning?"

    "Good good. How are you?"

    "God, just shoot me. Serious." She leans in close, pretending no one can hear. "I'm sick of this place."

That girl she works with, the one Alison says has a thing for me, Trisha, the one with a fat ass and no tits, she pops up from under the counter, arms loaded with coffee cups and stacks of java jackets that amazingly don't spill all over the place when she tilts this way and that, putting stuff here and there around the till.

I walk over to her. "Can I get a coffee?"

She laughs, gives me a wink while her fingers peck at the buttons on the register. "I don't know. Can you?"

"I want a medium."

"Room for cream?"

"No."

"No cream?"

"Nope."

"No sugar?"

"Naw."

"So, just.... black then?"

"Uh huh."

"Okay." Her voice turns to nearly inaudible mumbles as she turns around and fills a mug with coffee. "One black coffee it is then."

Alison picks up the rag, moves to another table, barely wiping it at all. I look out the window at the passing cars, Trisha sets the mug on the counter. "That's two dollars and..."

"I need it to go."

She stops, looks down at the mug and bumps her palm against her forehead. "Oh my god, that's right. I'm so sorry!"

She dumps the cup out in the sink, grabs a to go one, fills it and is all red faced when she rings it up. "Sorry. Mondays!"

Today is Friday. I smile, wrap my fingers around the warm cylinder of wax and paper, filled to the brim with boiling black caffeine. "That's okay."

Sinners Circle

Around noon Alison comes into my store and starts talking. I'm only listening to her body language. I can't hear what she's saying, over the pounding of the Witch Drums. I watch her eyes for Black Stars. I smile.

She smiles too. Her lips are moving but I can't hear what she's saying. I'm comfortable enough to smile again, which makes her blush, then turn on her heel and leave.

Absolutely nothing happens for the next four hours. I'm cleaning a display of Acryl dildos with a feather duster, thinking about how I'd once read somewhere that the term *dildo* originally referred to this dick shaped peg that sailors used to lock the oars on their boats, when I hear the entry bell ringing above the door.

I turn, and no kidding, in strolls a little girl with this older guy trailing behind her. The guy's got a sun hat on and one of those douchebag beards, the chin strap kind. He's clearly over forty, his gut is proof of that, and on top of everything else, he's wearing socks with sandals. The little girl bounces over to the movies.

I know I should do something, but I can't. I just can't stop staring, the feather duster hovering over the tips of all those dildos, I cannot believe what I am seeing.

The little girl picks up a movie, flips it over to look at the back. She tugs on the guy's shirt. "Get one with big dicks! Some big black dicks! I want to see some big cocks tonight!"

Blaine comes out of his office holding that clip chart, he sees me with my mouth hung open and looks over at the two. He stops in mid step, eyes popping out of his head, we both look at each other—the same look of horror on our faces.

The little girl picks up another movie. "They do facials in this one?" She's twisting a pig tail around her finger when I hear the bell above the door again. Two guys walk through the door, freezing a few paces in, then start shuffling backwards to leave. Blaine's whole face goes red and he charges up to the jerk in the sun hat with the chin strap rapist beard and slams his whole fist against the rack of DVDs.

"Hey! What the hell are you doing in here with a little girl, asshole? What the..." He looks down at her and stops shouting. His face goes redder than a burning tomato, his lips forming a huge *O*. The customers by the door, they move a little closer, I drop the duster when the little girl screams, throwing the movies onto the floor, "I'm *not* a *little girl*, you idiot! I'm a *fucking midget*!"

Blaine gives them free rentals for a month and lets the guy take home a pair of edible underwear, the girl gets a dildo on the house.

After they leave Blaine comes up to me shaking his head, "Huh.. well that was close. Hey, do you think midgets have tiny pussies?"

I think about that a lot actually. But, it's one of those facts I never bothered to learn. When I get health insurance, I'll get a doctor and I'll ask her. "Naw. I think they're kind of like the Elephant Man. In the sense that they're whole body is fucked up but their pussies are normal. I think midget guys have tiny dicks though."

He burps into a meat glove of a fist. It's twice as red as hamburger. "Joseph Merrick had a normal dick?"

"Yeah"

He's quiet for a second, fidgeting two fingers like he's thinking about something. "Could you imagine what it would look like if the Elephant Man had a baby with a midget?"

I smiled. I like, Blaine. He's a funny guy. "Well, if they can't cover the medical bills, they can just sell it as a football."

He doesn't laugh. He doesn't even twitch. He sighs, "Okay, well just tidy up a bit. I'll count till if you take out the trash."

I hate how vulnerable he makes me feel sometimes. "Wow! Really?"

"Yeah, I got some numbers I have to add from last night, balance some digits."

I sit down on the stool behind the counter. "Blaine, you *know* I can count till..."

He takes his hands out of his pockets, waves them and touches my arm, which sort of creeps me out. "No no, it's not that. I know you can be trusted on this shit, but I really do have to add some numbers up. To be honest..." He looks around the store again. "Just between you and me, I don't think the other guy who comes in nights is all that together, if you know what I mean?"

"Huh?"

"I think he's got some..." he taps his nostril, "... some habits and I doubt he's covering them all too well with his salary."

"Oh."

"Think he's got sticky fingers, and is dipping them in the cash register now and again."

"Oh."

He leans in a little and half whispers, "I think he's the reason we lost those gag balls, too."

"You think he's stealing stock?"

"Yeah, I do."

I shrug again and pretend that his point is really sinking in. "Yeah, I guess that makes sense."

"I got to keep an eye on him."

"Yeah, totally. Keep your eye on the creeps."

I swing the bags of trash into the alley dumpster out back, light a smoke and look at the passing helicopters shining their spot lights against the sides of glass buildings. I've never stolen cash from here, I don't think it's right. The girls I take home and get rid of, they've always got some cash on them, so I just take whatever they've got in their purses and that's always covered my extra expenses fine. However, I don't want Blaine to see me ringing in gag balls and dildos.

In the two years I've worked here he's told me a few times about girls wandering in and asking for me, and he's always had this lingering look in his eye whenever my personal life is brought up. I just try and keep that aspect of myself under wraps with him. Last thing I need is him asking me about my sex life and me having to think about drinking blood and sewing rats into women's stomachs after the orgasm. Well, I don't really mind thinking about that, just not while I'm at work with my horny middle-aged boss. I stop before heading back into the store and look at his truck. He's got a cool truck. It's an old nineteen seventy nine, Ford F one-fifty,.Free Wheel'n. Yellow with a shock of brown and maroon across the side. My favorite part about it though, is the antlers, the giant buck antlers mantled on the push bar bumper. I think it looks really cool.

I look at the glowing lights above the door. I don't blink my eyes and I stare into the red lights, trance-like. My mind floats through a sea of shadow and shouts in the distance. I'm thinking about Nazi's and cigarettes and Lilly. I see her milky skin and red lips, naked and puffing on a cigarette against red silk sheets. White curtains and an open window that sprays blue light under a brick view. Lilly throws me the Nazi salute and laughs and I am swallowed into her mouth.

I shake my head and cough. I blink, rub my eyes and think.

I think how I've never met the other guy who works here. I know it's him, me and some other guy who works part time nights here, I mean I've seen them once or twice, but we've never really spoken. Except for once when he needed me to hand him his jacket, but that's it.

I walk around the side of the building, kiss Lilly on the cheek and take her out for Greek food. She tells me about a friend of hers who hooks on the other side of town and is now missing.

Chapter 12

When I came home the front door to our trailer was open, just swinging on its hinges, banging lightly against the tin shell of our mobile home. Inside, the hideaway bed was tucked in, the drawers where full of my socks, the floor strewn with my dirty underwear, but all of mom's stuff was gone.

I slept on the floor because I couldn't pull out the bed; my arms weren't strong enough, so yeah, I slept on the floor for two days, the door open swinging in the rain and sun and clouded weather of those forty-eight hours. I missed school and had my first cigarette on the soggy carpet step, staring at the trailer adjacent to us, feeling nothing, not even moving the hair from between my lips when the wind blew it there.

The sleepy social worker showed up in the morning. The messy, drawn out bitch, yawned through sentences like, "Your mother is now a missing person." And, "Do you know if there is any coffee in here?"

She opened the cabinets, and when she saw there was only peanut butter and a mini box of Corn Flakes she shut them, asked me to move, pulled out the hideaway bed and collapsed onto it. "Nope, no coffee."

I just stared at her for a full ten minutes, her eyes closed, her lips moving in little gasps, like a fish pulled out of water and tossed onto the floor of a boat. When she woke up, she looked around, hands absent mindedly patting her bangs. "Ok, so you ready?"

The only thing I took out of that trailer was my Donkey Kong pajamas.

I spent the next four years in a foster home, sleeping in the same room with a deaf girl named Gina. She taught me sign language and how to dance to music by feeling the vibrations. I taught her how to make paper airplanes and toys out of twist ties. The first year I was there, she showed me pictures of her dead parents. The second year, she showed me how to read brail. The third year, she showed me how to eat pussy. And the fourth year she showed me a newspaper detailing the torture and death of an American citizen at the hands of eight children ranging in age between seven and twelve down in Mexico. The kids, all orphans, called themselves pirates. They sailed around the coasts of Mexico in stolen boats, robbing and looting from elderly store owners and lost tourists. The kids, they found a woman passed out drunk inside one of their hideouts, some abandoned shack in the middle of nowhere. The kids, the boys, they kept her there for over a week, locked in the cellar, beating her with chains, pushing pins in her arms and legs and leaving them there for a day or two. Then they raped her, starting out slow and curious, putting all kinds of things in her from around the house, the boat, their pockets. They pushed paperclips inside her urethra, forced crabs inside her vagina, and eventually made her eat their shit while they pulled all the hair out of her head with their sticky little hands. Those eight wetback throwaways broke her legs and all her teeth. The newspaper said when the police found her she didn't have a face and one of her arms was missing. The kids only got caught because after the lady was dead the older boys started raping the youngest one and making him eat their feces. The little boy ran away, got taken in to the cop shop by some day sailing tourists. At the police station, the little smudge agreed to show authorities where the other 'pirates' were hiding. When the cops got there, they found the boys, beating and raping each other. Shoving handfuls of shit down each other's throats.

Two weeks after Gina showed me that newspaper, she was eating me out in the bathtub when my foster mom knocked on the door. "You girls are too old to be in the bath together..."

I was wearing my bathrobe walking past the kitchen, drinking a coke when my foster mom said, "Amanda, can you come in here, please?"

Two police officers were sitting at the dinner table while my foster mom, Debbie, was crying into a dish rag. This first cop to speak, he looked like the kind of guy you could slap in the mouth and he would think it was his fault and probably apologize for getting in the way of your hand. He looked like a wimpier Don Knotts, like his legs were made of wet bread and his spine was nothing more than a cord of garden worms. This wimp looked at the other police man who stood up, took off his cowboy hat and stared at his shoes, shoes that I couldn't see, because the breakfast table was covering his legs.

"Amanda, Miss, could you come here for a minute please? We'd like to talk to you."

I walked over to the table, put my coke down, Debbie moved the can away from the ledge. I remember thinking the policeman with the cowboy hat should really have put the fuckin' thing back on because he was so damn bald without it. The cowboy cop took out a newspaper tucked in his arm pit and unrolled it on the table. "Miss, I believe we've found your mother, Francis Troy."

Sims

The picture of the woman on the gray paper, printed in halftone, she sat in the living room of our trailer for five years, on top of the TV watching my mother and I watch whatever was on. I was sitting in the shopping cart chewing gum and fucking up my shoe laces when she got the picture taken at Walmart. When she got the prints back, she spilled gin all over them except for the one we put up on top of the TV.

Debbie, sobbing into that old shitty rag that smells like garbage, she isn't sad, she's just trying to make the story better. Trying to make herself part of something half the country will hear about. The bald cowboy is blowing bad breath up my nose as his mouth contorts around the words, "Francis Troy has been identified as the victim of a child gang slaying down in Mexico. All suspects have been apprehended. The State would be willing to pay your way to see the case in court, if you're willing to attend the trial."

There is a moment in our lives when things change. For a lot of people this happens after death. Their ways of thinking, their views of others, their awareness is brought to an entirely different plateau. But for some, when this happens in the midst of life, the reality of objects, others, what is being said, become crystal clear. I saw the man in the cowboy hat wiggling his tongue around words he didn't fully understand. I saw the age on his face, the wrinkles on Debbie's face. I noticed she had her nice slippers on, I noticed the wimp with the gun and the shiny badge pinned to his shirt didn't really give a fuck. His eyes, like two Black Stars.

Even if he did give a fuck, he couldn't bring my mom back. He wouldn't be putting those eight Mexican kids in prison. Even if he had the best intentions in the world, he couldn't do shit about anything. And because of this, in reality, he held no honest authority.

What was coming out of the cowboy's mouth, they were just words. Sentences in fragments that I couldn't hear. I couldn't put together. I reached for my coke, when I dropped it in the kitchen I just kept walking until my back was against my bedroom wall, my bum on the carpet.

Sinners Circle

I heard words floating through the door, words like "Francis" and "Marcy" and "raped by cousin." Excited voices popping, "both runaways from Mennonite commune," "Francis kept the baby... Amanda." I could hear Gina splashing around in the tub, her fingers skipping across the water.

Whoever was in charge, whoever's finger hovered over the button of my fate, decided it was in my best interest to stay with Debbie and Gina until Marcy could fix up a suitable place for me.

While I waited at Debbie's for Marcy, I filled the big plastic laundry basket with water, I put the cat in it, and held the lid shut until the bucket stopped shaking. I broke into my neighbor's house and stole his pornography. I beat a rabbit to death with a hammer and pushed pencils up our other neighbor's dog's ass. I lit the garage on fire and kicked a two-year-old in the back at the supermarket when no one was looking. And I never got caught or blamed for any of this stuff. I could literally break a cats front legs and everyone would say, "Aww, there's that girl we saw in her pajamas crying on the news about her deadbeat murdered mother." When Gina would eat me out, I would pull the sides of her hair hard enough until her little deaf screams came out in high whistles. She'd spend all day hiding away from me, crying and saying she was sorry and she loved me. She'd hug me and wave her arms around saying, "Don't you love me anymore?" I didn't even use my hands to tell her I couldn't feel anything with her anymore, I walked into her until she was against the wall and our faces where too close for her to read my lips. I told her I didn't want to fuck her if I couldn't put my fist in her. She went away crying, coming back, her hands flailing around, telling me she was trying to get herself to open enough. She never could and the last night I was there, I snuck over to her bed while she was asleep, put all my weight on her chest and fisted her until the sides of her pillow were soaked with tears, her lips shredded from biting down so hard.

The next morning, that same sleepy social worker came over and asked Debbie for coffee and then she drove me to Marcy's house. The house my dad owned and left to the commune at his passing. They in turn gave it to Marcy, this house, the one I live in now, 16 years later.

Chapter 13

This morning I'm woken up by some kids singing 'Over the Rainbow' as they walk by my house. I march to the front door and yell at them to shut up. Then I turn on the radio. Talking Heads 'Psycho Killer' is playing. I turn the volume all the way to the right and shout along to the words, "Je me lance, vers la gloire, okay, we are vain and we are blind, I hate people when they're not polite."

Around eleven I've finished my coffee, I'm scratching my crotch and thinking about wandering over to Alison's and getting another cup. But that can only happen if some jerk-off doesn't come in here in the next five minutes. Blaine is in his office, door wide open, chatting on the phone, his voice getting real loud every time it's his turn to speak. He's talking about road trips and Chlamydia. From way up here at the front of the store I can hear him tell the telephone he picked crabs out of his pubes and was scared at first that one would scuttled down his pee hole.

I toss the empty cup into the trash, stand and dig around the counter for the 'back in five minutes' sign as soon as he shouts, "...Oh, I know all the faces there..." His feet clapping the cement flooring of his office.

I can only imagine the kind of guy on the other end of the line, I mean what kind of weirdo talks this long to another man on the telephone? Let alone the subject matter, such senseless banter as this. So, I get up to get coffee and ditch for a few when Lilly comes limping through the door, her eyes all swollen up, lip split, she's got an arm wrapped around her ribs. Her shirt torn from collar to midriff, scratched knees weak and shaking in broken heels. "Amanda..."

I barely catch her before she collapses forward, "Lilly... what happened?"

Before she can speak she just comes apart, crying and writhing in my arms, feet scraping the carpet. "They jumped me, I got out of the car and..." I can tell the way her wrist is twisted when she goes to wipe the snot from her nose that her radius and ulna are fractured if not completely broken. "...two guys in the fucking back, they were just watching me and him in the front... fuckers got me in the alley. The car, the guy in the car just drove away. I think..."

Blaine is laughing in the back, banging his feet on the floor, his voice getting hoarse, "...feeble camouflage!"

I pick Lilly up, push the door open and carry her to Alison's work. Trisha is flipping through the newspaper, circling ads when I kick the door open and lay Lilly down on the floor. She screams, a few customers stand up, hover over and don't leave until I push them out. I grab the phone, Trisha tries pulling it away from me, "What are you doing? This is a *business* line."

"What's going on? Holy fuck!" Alison grabs the phone from Trisha, dials nine-one-one. "There's a girl! A fucking girl looks like she's going to die..."

"Amanda?" Lilly's twisted little arms are waving in the air above her. I grab a cup of water and wrap my arms around her shoulders, I can feel her getting colder and in the eighteen minutes it takes for the ambulance to arrive I never move my face from her hair.

When the paramedics load her up on the stretcher and all the onlookers watch the ambulance speed off, Blaine is standing there, arms crossed, staring at me. "You left the store unattended."

I look down at myself, the front of my white t shirt is all wet, scrunched up and smeared in blood.

"... and you've got blood on your shirt."

"She might die."

"You should've told me."

"You were on the phone."

He sighs, "Someone could have come in and taken shit. You have to let me know if you're..."

"She was gonna *die,* asshole!"

"Hey!"

"Fuck off!"

I push past him and head back to the store.

"You can't talk to me like that, I'll..."

"Fuck off!"

He follows me in, points at my shirt again. "I can't let you work in that."

"You telling me to go home?"

"No....I just..." He unfolds his arms, scratches the back of his neck and waves a hand towards his office. "I got a bunch of playboy tank tops in the back. Find one that fits and come back to the front."

His little janitor closet turned office smells like wet paper and old garlic. I'm digging through a cardboard box, *titty tops* scrawled in red marker on the side in Blaine's handwriting. The office is so damn small I knock over a stack of magazines piled beside the desk. I quickly slip on a black tank top. The Playboy bunny stamped to the front in gaudy rhinestones. I bend down to pick up the skin rags. Half of them are water logged, pages swollen. Under the desk it reeks like piss. I'm just grabbing the last magazine off the floor when I notice the phone cord isn't plugged into the jack. I look on top of the desk and see the receiver off the hook. I plug it back in, stand up and push call history. According to this, the last phone call was made today at six AM. One missed incoming at nine o'clock.

"Amanda?" Blaine is shouting from the front of the store.

"Yeah?"

I unplug the phone again and lay the receiver back on its side. There's five long black strands of hair laid out beside the keyboard of his computer. I touch my scalp, pluck out a hair and hold it up to the bulb on the ceiling.

Blaine yells from the front of the store. "You finding everything ok?"

I'm squinting one eyed to make sure I'm right, that I'm positively correct.

"Yeah... I found everything."

I walk back to the till. "You ok, Blaine?"

He shakes his head, rubs his belly and laughs. "Sorry for all the rags in there."

He scratches the back of his neck again and points at my top. "Looks nice."

"Ok."

"Well, I'm gonna head off to McDonalds. You want anything?"

"No."

"Come on, you look thin. I'll bring you back something."

"No, I'm not hungry."

He shrugs. "Fine. Go for your lunch when I get back."

He goes to his office, gets his coat and leaves out the back door. The second he leaves I crack my neck, grab the sandwich out of my lunch bag and look through the newspaper to see if the remains of the jogger have been discovered yet. I'm sort of pissed when I see, after two goddamn weeks, there still hasn't been a missing person notice yet. I wipe the crumbs off my stomach and wave at Trisha when she gets in her car outside the store. She holds a thumb up to her ear, a pinkie to her mouth. I smile and swallow the rest of my sandwich.

Chapter 14

"That chick." Alison is pointing at a group of people bobbing their heads at a table. I crane my neck, I don't see anything except wig hair and black clothing. She pulls me next to her, aiming her arm like a rifle. "That one, that chick right there."

"Okay."

"You see her?"

She's pointing at a tired looking thirty something, slug lips and low tits. Bad sweater, cheap jeans. "Sure."

She doesn't lower her flesh rifle, just keeps on pointing it straight at cheap jeans. "She looks like Octomom. Except, minus the sort of looking like Angelina Jolie part."

I laugh, peel the label off my beer and scatter the shreds of paper across my lap, her lap. "I saw a dyke down here once who looked like Dan Aykroyd."

"Gross."

Karl and some scrawny wired looking fag sit down, I take a shot glass from him and he rolls his eyes, digs in his pocket for baggies of meth.

"Yeah it was gross."

Karl wraps an arm around Alison and scratches his nose. "What was gross?"

The skinny fag, he's pulling out little paper envelopes, tiny plastic bags, turning them upside down in his palm and then tossing them on the floor. After a full minute of watching him do this I poke him in the arm, "You got a name?"

He looks at me like I've slapped his baby. "Don't fucking *touch* me! I don't wanna drop this shit." He even shakes his hand a little for emphasis.

Karl points a beer bottle at him, "Oh Amanda this is..."

I roll a wad of phlegm from the back of my throat and launch a perfect gob onto this skinny fuckers cheek. "You got a name?"

Even with a ball of spit and throat gunk dripping down his cheek, he doesn't move, just keeps pulling out flaps of meth, coke, who knows what he's got pinched in there. Whatever it is, it's probably so cut its more cupcake mix than drugs. He just stares in his hand, dumping empty little bags and throwing them at his shoes. "Ronnie."

Alison shakes her head and tosses Ronnie a napkin. He doesn't touch it but flinches as it lands by his hand.

Karl looks over at the table, the one where Octomom is, or was. "Where's that cunty waitress? The blonde one... the one with the..." He cups an invisible tit.

I shrug. Ronnie doesn't do anything, he's dumping more baggies into a small mountain of powder growing in his palm. Thing is though, he's sweating almost as fast as the mound is growing, salty perspirant quickly dissolving his drugs into goop. I'd say something, but I am sort of curious to see if the chemicals will absorb into his system through his skin.

Alison looks at me, then at Ronnie, then at me, then at Karl. Her eyes wide, her mouth pulled down, she doesn't look very attractive. "You guys are *fucking* kidding me!"

She does the look around thing again. I just keep shrugging and Karl

Sims

doesn't even notice she's mad until she punches him in the arm, hard. "You *fucks*! She was *murdered*! It was on the news and everything. Last night was some fund raiser where half the profit from drinks went to her family..."

Ronnie slams a palm of wet drugs into his mouth and licks white slime dripping down his wrist. Karl looks at Alison, Karl looks at me, Alison looks at me. Alison says, "Amanda, didn't you sleep with her once or something?"

Ronnie is licking pigeon shit amphetamines from between his fingers, his eyes rolling like goddamn pool balls between us. I crack my neck, brush some of the peeled beer label scraps off my lap, "Well, I...."

"Oh my... *fuck*..." Ronnie, his whole face goes beat red, then totally pale and then hits the table. White drool pooling out the side of his mouth. It looks like an un ending stream of semen. From the way his body isn't moving, the rim of his lips tight and grey, eyes locked open you don't need to be a doctor to know he's having a heart attack.

Karl plays hero, he tells everyone to call an ambulance, he says he's a nurse and helps a drag queen, who flashes his MD ID around, save Ronnie's worthless life. The ambulance comes, takes Ronnie away, Karl goes with Dr. Drag, and when the lights turn back off and the music starts up again, it's just me and Alison. We do shots at the bar and I try talking about movies I've seen lately, but Alison won't talk about anything except Lilly and Ronnie and then eventually how much I should give Trisha a call.

"She likes you, she really likes you." She's got tears in her eyes and her hand never leaves my leg when she's saying all this. Every time she says 'likes you' her fingers get tense and it makes me really wet when she's crying on my shoulder in the taxi home because I can feel her breath on my ear. When we're just about at my house, she puts an arm across my stomach and swallows my earlobe.

And when I take her home and fuck her, it's not because I'm a bad friend, it's because I'm a bad person. And I don't even think about Karl across the city, breathing life into some gay stranger as I take off all of his girlfriend's clothes, keeping my mouth moving over hers so she can't voice any second thoughts. I don't think about our long-standing friendships because Alison has this really tight pussy and she doesn't tell me to stop when I can tell it's hurting her.

I fall asleep as the sun rises and when I wake up, Alison is standing over me half naked and wearing that jogger's *University of Oklahoma* sweat shirt. She's holding a plate of toast and scrambled eggs. She kisses my forehead, sits down on the bed and hands me the plate but not the fork, because she's drumming it on her bare knees. "Look, I don't regret last night or anything but, let's just keep this between us, ok?"

I smile. "Yeah, ok."

"Thanks."

Chapter 15

It's BlackOut. I'm in the park, on the grass, eyes to the sky watching Black Stars Rise.

Towering cumulus, black as smoke, rolls swiftly overhead. My mind drifts to the depths of Demhe. Across Hali. And over the gates of The Lost City.

I had painted my face white. I do that sometimes. When I go walking at night. I stand in front of the mirror in my bathroom and finger-paint my face white. My entire face. So there isn't any possible place for shadow to stay.

I'm standing close to the tree line for nearly forty-five minutes before a group of men jog by, stop at the fountain, and start sucking each other's dicks.

Ugh. Men are so lame.

I walk back home and wander into the backyard. I climb the staircase at the back of the house. It leads onto a patio with a sliding glass door where I can enter the house. I get to the top but I don't go in. I stand outside, on the patio and look in. The house is dark except for the light on the TV. The ever-changing color is blasting the outline of my aunt's silhouette. She's sitting in her arm chair, in front of the TV. I stand there, motionless, watching her. I remain through *Jeopardy*, one breaking news story. It's about Lilly.

They're splashing her face all over the news. I silently slide the glass door open and slip behind Marcy. The reporter says, "…heard screaming through the streets. This is, Camilla Castaigne reporting. Steven?"

Some guy came on to thank me for tuning in. Then *The Price is Right* blared across the screen.

I looked down at Marcy. She was fidgeting. I felt my hands fill with blood. My heart stared pounding. My chest started throbbing. My eyes flamed with tears. I flexed my fingers and blinked some paint off my eyelashes. I licked my lips and made up my mind to strangle Marcy when she got up to go to bed. I don't know if I'll kill her. I don't *want* her to die. I just want to strangle her unconscious.

My spine felt a rush of tingles. My clit started to throb. The soothing remedy of rage, creeping down my neck. Dark blood pumping through my veins. My blood is thicker when I'm angry. I bleed less.

I stood behind her, waiting for her to stand. I *needed* her to stand or else I wouldn't have anything to attack. So, I waited. I waited through 22 whole minutes of crap and trash TV only to see I'd zoned out again, and Marcy was fast asleep.

My shoulders slumped. I turned around and left out the sliding door. I shut it then descended the stairs, rounded to the front of the house and went through the front door into my place.

I sat against my bed for a long time, looking at pictures on the floor. I have six pictures with my mom. Four of them from the same year. The year before she went missing. In all of them, Mom and I are in the woods. Only one of them has Mom, me and Marcy in it. I'm a baby, I'm in a jolly jumper and both of them are playing with me. I asked Marcy once who had taken this photo. She said, "We used a timer."

I remember feeling disappointed with that. I wanted there to be some great mystery for me to follow. Maybe I could follow it and it would lead me to some exotic place and I'd find mom and she wasn't actually dead.

I didn't tell Marcy that part. I didn't want to make her sad.

I put the picture in a box, closed the lid and slid it under my bed.

Owls hoot outside my window. There's a windchime outside my door.

I slide into bed, slip naked around on new sheets. As I drift asleep, I am glad I didn't hurt Marcy tonight.

Maybe I'll cook her dinner later this week.

Chapter 16

"She developed an allergy to cats when she was young, but she always loved them." Karl is cradling one of those Fur Real cats, you know, those toys moms buy for their kids when they get bored of their real living breathing, shitting house pets. He's petting the robot kitten, flicking the flaps of fabric sewn to its scalp as ears. In some spots the fur been trimmed right down to the plastic body. What used to be white hair is now all grey. One of the back legs is busted and there's gum stuck to the underbelly, keeping the battery case in place. "She spent all day winding these fuckers up or pluggin' in batteries to keep 'em going. She had about six dozen of these..." He pokes the eye, grabs a calico and lifts the tail looking for the crotch. "... Yup, at *least* that many."

I lean against the desk, the one with all the FUCK YOUs cut into it. "What brought her in here?"

He laughs, tosses me the bubble gum bellied kitty. "Neighbors. Apparently, she was busted, breaking into a little girl's bed room next door's one night." He yawns, which makes me yawn and my eyes water while he mumbles on, "Kid screamed so the parents called the cops, naturally."

"What?"

He shrugs. "Yeah, she'd cut half her own ear off that night as well. Blood all over the place." His finger snips his earlobe. "To look like one of these things." He prods the plastic ribs of the calico, Velcro stomach opened up. This cat must've been one of those toys that came pregnant in the box, kittens sold separately. Kids could play and replay the joys of pregnancy until they got bored with the miracle of life and those tiny cloth kittens with retractable eyelids wound up in the garbage can or lost in some dark and forgotten corner of the house. "When they brought her in here, she was saying she didn't think they'd catch her, because she was invisible."

I put the cat back on the desk. Karl drags a hand down its back. "True story."

"What's that?" I point at a deflated blow up doll on the bottom shelf.

He turns around, smiles, and hikes a thumb behind him. "Oh *that's* the Queen. Dennis, you know the 'King of France' in here, yeah, that's his lady. That's *La Reine.*"

"Hot."

He laughs, small bits of spit flying off his lips and landing on my arm. "Yeah, what a fucker."

I crack my knuckles, trace a finger along the obscenities carved into the table.

Karl looks at his watch. "Oh shit, I gotta go, Amanda, I'll catch you later."

We walk down that awful hallway, this time the screaming is coming from the rooms on the other side, while total silence weighs on the other. Karl pats my back in the main lobby and waves a hand over his shoulder. "See ya later."

I go over to the apple box library and dig through the *Archies* until I find a water damaged digest featuring Cherry Blossom. I sit down on that awful couch and move my eyes back and forth from Cherry's tits to the nurse's station. One of the cool things about Karl is he's a Sabrina man, you know, that white haired teenage witch bitch. I'm a Cherry Blossom girl. Neither of us are Betty and Veronica people, and that's rarer than you'd think. It's these small differences that really matter.

Cherry is half way to the mall when out of the corner of my eye that big lug from the porn store, the one with pockets that looked like huge swaying tumors from all the shit he was trying to steal, appears out of nowhere and sits down beside me. He's thumbing a dog-eared bible and I'm not even kidding when I say he's got dish towels stitched together and safety pinned to the back of his Goldberg t-shirt. He opens the book but stares at me from the corner of his eye.

The lumpy pad of comic pulp in my hands shows Cherry laughing at a pair of boots. I turn to the big tumor thief and smack my lips together, "Hi. I'm Amanda."

He looks up from the bible he's pretending to read. "I'm Dennis..."

"Hi Dennis."

He looks down at the carpet, tucks his slippered feet tight into the couch then closes his eyes and asks, "Have you accepted Jesus as your personal savio..."

"Are you a rapist?"

His eyes snap open, breath caught in his throat.

I look him in the eye and smile. "It's not like she ever said *no*... but that doll you're fucking, it never really said *yes* either, did it? I mean, masturbation is a sin, too. And if you've accepted Christ..." I point at his bible. "And you're *still* doing it... I'm sorry, Dennis, but..." I lean in a little bit. "You're going to hell."

His face does this funny little dance between screwing up into tears, getting angry, back to crying, then straight to tomato red. He jumps up, that half destroyed bible flying to the ceiling and like all great things, falling to the floor faster than it rose. "Blasphemy! Satan! Satan! Satan!"

When he shouts like this, I can see all the veins in his neck and forehead. *"Do you know who I am?"*

While a nurse shoos him off for shots and straight coats, I slip in the coma ward and wander around until I find Lilly's room.

She's lying in bed, hooked up to all sorts of breathing machines and tubes running fluids into her. I'm sort of moved when I see the blankets are tucked in at her arm pits.

The clipboard swinging at the edge of her bed tell me this is Lilith Kimberly Wahlund DOB: Feburary 21st 1994.

Upon arrival she had severe internal bleeding, ecchymosis of the liver, multiple cigarette burns to the left foot and calf, damage to the Achilles tendon, possibility of temporal brain damage. Condition: unconscious/responsive to heat.

At the bottom of the page is a signature from RN Sophia Harris. Says here Sophia checked on Lilly twenty minutes ago. I pull up a chair beside Lilly's bed and pet her head. I kiss her fingernails and watch her breathe for a few minutes. I stand, press my fingertips into the glass pane and pull them into towards my palm so there's a streak that looks like a flower; I drag a finger down each center, stemming the posy. The sun comes out behind a sky scraper, shining directly into my eyes so that I'm forced to look away. I turn back to Lilly and bend to kiss her eyelids. As I pull away, I gently bite a strand of her hair and chew it as I walk back down the hall and out into the world.

Chapter 17

"There's more 22's over there. You missed them." She slaps my hand away before my brush touches the cardboard. "*Different* brush, *please!*"

I drop my brush in a glass, purple bleeding into the warm water making it look like My Little Pony took a piss test. Marcy waves a few fingers over to the palette of acrylic paint smeared onto a dinner plate. "Pass me the orange."

I pass her the plate, get a new brush and swirl the tip into some robin's egg blue. "Are you even allowed to be getting help with these?"

She rolls her eyes, "As long as it's *me* telling you what to do and you are here with *me* I don't see how I can get disqualified."

A brass plaque commending her victory in the 1994 state Paint-by-Numbers Contest, hangs beside a framed Last Supper. At the bottom is a green ribbon: Participation nineteen-ninety.

This year the painting requirement for the competition is Mother Mary. Judges will look at all five hundred paint-by-number portraits, eventually presenting a plaque to the winner and pinning ribbons to the chests of the losers.

Marcy is the most militant paint by numbers artist on the planet. If the colors go outside the thin black lines of the assigned number, she's prone to emotional collapse. So far, we've had to start over twice.

We sit in complete silence. Finally, she leans back, closing her eyes and motions for me to take away the plate of paint. She wheels herself over to the kitchen. "I'm ready for clean up."

I soak a rag, wash her fingertips and arms, carefully rubbing away any bits of paint on her skin. While I wash her face with warm water she asks me, "You talk to any of those boys?"

I wipe a glob of ivory white off her cheek and toss the rag into the sink. "Boys?"

She wheels back a bit and rolls over to the couch. "Yeah. You know, *men*."

"No, sorry... No. I haven't"

"Well, if the guys you work with are such dolts then why don't you try getting friendly with some of the customers?"

I think about Rick finger banging the silicone cunts on the shelf, Dennis raping his inflatable Queen of France and crying about going to Hell. I think about the midget and the creep who stood beside her. I think about Trisha, I think about the dildos I stole and I think about hiding them *inside* Trisha. I think about Lilly, I think about her little burned feet and I think about murdering Blaine with a baseball bat while he's masturbating.

"No, they aren't anything to write home about, Marcy. So, *bringing* them here... it's not an option. You wouldn't like them anyway."

She turns around to face me, her eyes heavy with insecurities, "Why? Why wouldn't *I* like them?"

I run the dish towel under some warm water to get all the paint out. "Because you just wouldn't."

She turns back to her TV staring at it for a good minute before turning *The Price is Right* on. I clean up her painting messes, do her dinner dishes and ask if she needs help going to the bathroom. She doesn't say anything so I open the door to the stairs that go down to my floor.

She says, "You're ashamed of me."

Sinners Circle

Bob Barker asks America to please spay or neuter our pets.

I turn to her and say, "No Marcy, you would be ashamed of *me*." I'm not good at this, considering others people's feelings is always a shot in the dark with me. I think that if I can have a loving relationship with a family member, then I must be doing fine with my daily life. I never really mean what I say. I just don't care. I want to go downstairs and kill myself.

As I'm walking down the stairs to my suite, that cuckoo clock clucks three pm. I grab my wrist watch off the back of my couch and call Karl.

Neither of us have work that day so he comes over and smoke pot and talk about Hitler because, today is his birthday. Alison calls and says she'll be here in forty-five minutes. So, while we wait, we listen to Marilyn Manson, and talk about sex while I read the newspaper.

Karl is saying something about beautiful monsters. I don't know, I'm not listening. I'm looking at an article.

A gunman was killed after shooting four police officers and two bystanders. Nobody died except for him.

I look up from the newspaper Karl says, "In Rollingstone, Marilyn Manson said he experimented with pain killers to test his pain threshold by inserting sewing needles under his fingernails."

I read an article about how gun control will now be looked at as a form of treason in, Sacramento. The article quotes a voicemail left by an anonymous caller, "Guns are not for hunting. When will you people figure that out? Guns are for hunting down politicians when they steal your rights away through tyranny. Hello!"

I hear Alison come through the door and say hello but I don't respond because a man in Apple Valley California, lit himself on fire on his ex-girlfriend's front lawn and suffered critical injuries. Someone driving by saw the flames, pulled over and rolled them out.

I wonder if somewhere out there, there's a man who is doing the same thing I am, in burn units and comma wards. But to men.

I laugh and close the newspaper. "Hey, Alison!"

Alison is saying something about nothing so, I interrupt her. "How's

Sims

Ronnie doing, Karl?"

He shrugs. "I don't know."

I wish they'd leave so, I could just go in my room and listen to David Bowie and be alone.

I walk through them and into the living room. My face feels like jelly, my heart is racing as my fingers fumble across the stereo buttons. I pre-load Bowie for my days off, my stereo is the best, I stole it from a porch down the street. It's top of the line.

My anxiety ebbs, in flowing ribbons of rosy pink relief as Bowie breathes life into the world, 'It's a godawful small affair...' Cuts through the room and settles over me in a fine mist.

I am floating in the most peculiar way, indeed. When I turn around both of them are gone. I check all the rooms. They've vanished.

I shake my head, I must've been sleep walking and dreaming and just woke up. I look down, I'm still in my clothes I put on this morning. I pinch myself. It hurts.

I rub my eyes and sigh. I feel my chest burn the way it always starts to burn just before I begin to cry.

I walk to my bedroom and am about to get back into bed, in case this *is* a dream, when the music in the living room shuts off and I hear Alison yelling, "*Hurry* up! We've been waiting in the car for like ten minutes!"

I look over at the clock beside my bed and I can read the numbers. This isn't a dream. I need psychiatric help.

I yell, "Coming!", then duck into the bathroom and flush the toilet. I run the sink for five seconds then when Alison can see me, I wipe my hands on my jeans like I'm drying them in a hurry.

I get in the front seat of Alison's car. We're going in Alison's car because Karl's car is a piece of shit and it's dirty. And we aren't taking my Jeep because I don't want to waste gas on these people. Paying at the pump is highway robbery.

Sinners Circle

Karl wants the front seat but Karl doesn't get the front seat because he's a fucking idiot. And when he asks why I'm sitting in the front seat, that's exactly what I tell him.

Palm trees bend behind us in rearview mirrors. I roll down the windows. Purple ocean waves, tinted sunlight through pollution. I close my eyes and feel an electricity sting inside of me. My blood mutated into a solvent of pure energy, a liquid worm squirming through my entire body secreting divine euphoria.

I never ask where we're going. I like to see how unaware my friends are. Everything is great for about five minutes, then we pull into a gas station and the mundaneness of the task knocks the worm out of me and I'm irritated and no longer in bliss.

I sigh and look over at Alison going into the gas station, I turn around until I see Karl and grunt in frustration, banging the back of my head on the car seat because, I can't masturbate with him here.

He says something but I don't care. I don't hear him, he doesn't matter. I get out of the car and hope I don't look creepy as I stretch my legs. I dunno, I'm always worried that I look creepy out in public. I don't want to be *that* guy, ya know?

Alison is talking to the gas station attendant and buying water. She is so slow she would wear the patience out of, Jesus.

A million years later, Alison gets back in the car and drives a stone throw from the gas station before making a sharp turn into a tiny parking lot. She kills the engine and the two of them got out of the car.

Trisha is there and the sun is setting.

When I get out of the car, Alison says, "We're here! Sorry we took so long Trish but..."

Karl pulls on the hem of my t-shirt. I turn around and he shoves bags that I don't want to carry, into my arms. He says, "Follow them down the beach. " He uses his chin to point at Alison and Trisha. "I can carry the rest."

Sims

I want to tell you that Trisha was all over me and I pushed her off and was too cool for everything. But that didn't happen. Trisha kept her distance from me and talked about boys.

We drank beer and Alison saw a turtle but it turned out to just be trash and as we were leaving a car pulled over and a young woman toppled out of the passenger door. The driver shouted, "You bit my fuck'n dick!" Then drove away. As she stood up and saw us standing there, the girl said "Don't judge!" Then ran away. Trisha put a hand to her heart and Alison looked like she was about to cry. Karl and I laughed. I wish I owned a video camera.

On the drive home, Trisha sits in the front, Karl drives and Alison and I have the back seat. Trisha keeps talking about boys.

She's a stupid fucking bitch and I want to stab her to death.

Karl and Alison get in a fight about something, I don't care. I'm looking out the window. Sure are a lot of old people walking around pretty late. Maybe they all have dementia. Who cares.

When we pull up to my house, Alison gets out of the car and slams the door. She tells Karl to go fuck himself then follows me inside.

She hugs me a lot and we drink beer until three in the morning. Around two she starts tonging my mouth and we take a shower together. She's straight to the point which is great because my clit had been throbbing all night and I was ready for it. So she sucked my clit in the shower and moaned and told me how great my body was.

When we got in my bed I started eating her pussy but she was limp and passing out. I was curving my tongue around the bottom of her vagina when she puked. Then she gargled. Then she puked again. Then she thrashed.

I sucked her clit and closed my eyes. I thought of fire and swords. I felt my clit throb to the pounding of the Witch Drums which beat soft then hard then not at all then too much.

My hands slithered to her slender neck. It was full and bouncing between gags that rhythmed, what must be to her, this living nightmare. Like invisible macabre ribbons. Happy Birthday, goodbye.

Would you believe me if I told you that I am a good person?

I sit up and turn Alison on her side. She vomits like soup. I make sure her eyes are closed then I play with it. I taste it. Then I make sure she's okay.

I lay down in her warm puddle of milky yogurt. She is so precious. I kiss her lips. I push my tongue into the back of her throat and swallow any bits I find in there. Large or small. I take them away. She is okay now. She will live.

I lay next to her and check her vitals. I make sure she's breathing and place pillows beside her so she can't roll over anymore and choke. Then I pat her head.

She's asleep.

Chapter 18

Karl drops a cup of coffee on the counter, half of it running under the cash register. "Drink."

I cough into my fist, look around the store and sigh. "I don't think I'm happy."

"Who is?"

He pulls a few pussy pocket key chains off the displays and shoves his finger inside until they break. I crack my neck and scratch my stomach, my mind drifting towards maggots. I sigh. "Do you think some people, they're just different right... and maybe they are just meant to be alone. Like forever and like, that's how they're supposed to be. That's their role and shit, yeah?"

Two fingers popping through two key chain pussies, he looks up. "What?"

"I just mean—"

"No, I missed the whole thing. What were you saying?"

Some fat asshole who's been pacing in front of the store all morning catches me looking at him. He looks up and then runs out the store. I can see where he stops, panting in front of traffic.

I look at Karl, he's pulling torn bits of rubber finger pussy off the keychain. "I'm dying inside."

He nods "Huh, I've never seen it. Is it good?"

"Only in the jungle."

A tiny clitoris flies into the counter Karl points at it. "Do I have to pay for these?" The two dangling vaginas, they remind me of the girl I left in my basement. I sewed a rat inside her to see what it would do. After two weeks I thought it was dead, but then it came nibbling out of her vagina. "No."

He smiles, says something about pants. I tap my feet to the Witch Drum, my heartbeat keeping sync. My mind travels through twisted sewer canals. Stony and underground. I see rats squeezing themselves out through a single pipe, onto toxic grass by a river somewhere. I think of the rats wriggling themselves out of the rotten vagina on the girl back at my place. I wonder if there is to be any symbolism to be gathered from that? At the thought of a potential possibility, I get a glorious rush of ecstasy. I give Karl a hug before he leaves, pat his shoulder and everything until Blaine comes out of his shitty little office to talk about nickels and dimes.

Blaine shows me a piece of paper, something about customer complaints or whatever. He shows me a list of lost and misplaced items and then he tells me about the importance of cleanliness for the sake of our female customers and then he stomps back into his office and I hear the click of the door being locked from inside.

I don't know why I'm still at this job. But what else would I do? Work at a coffee shop? Waitress? At least here I can steal gag balls and dildos and never be suspected for it. I'd quit, but I have no desire to work anywhere else, just as I have no desire to work here. When I started working here I was earning eleven dollars an hour, mostly because I was working nights, because we stay open twenty-four seven on weekends. After about a year I was going to go work at a shipping company but when I told Blaine I was quitting, he insisted on upping my salary. Now I make eighteen dollars and seventy-five cents every sixty minutes and mostly work day shifts. I have every second weekend off and I get three-day weekends. Blaine said it's because sales double on my shift and that he'd "have such a hard time finding another girl as pretty as I am."

I guess I stay because the money isn't that bad. I also don't have to pay rent as Marcy owns the house, and when she dies the inheritance

Sims

moves onto me. So, it's not that bad, I mean it gives me good stories to tell. But after those stories entertain you for five minutes, don't forget that I have to go *live* that shit. It gets dull.

I do, however, have the satisfaction of the upper hand in a way. For example, a man comes in here trying to buy the sickest, dirtiest rotten shit that can be legally sold and distributed within the United States. He comes in here with such high hopes, but goes home with *Anal Invaders* or *The Fist Time: Volume four*. He may get lucky with *Choked Sluts 7*, but I know that tape will only go so far and then end. So, I am satisfied with the fact that I have over a dozen snuff films labeled only by snips of hair glued to the cassette. Red heads, blondes, brunettes, but mostly just black hair. It feels good to know that nowhere in the entire world is a collection like mine.

Maybe that's why I stay. I'm a silent overlord, secretly gloating in the faces of all those flabby cowards who come wandering in here all alone, pathetic and horny.

Chapter 19

"Two years ago, Teresa Whitford painted Jesus Christ's face black. Out of all the entries, hers was the only one with the Negro skin. It lost yeah; it got taken down before the judges even saw it. She was banned from ever competing in the Paint by Numbers States contest for life. But Teresa is such a kind lady, so she came back to watch the next year's contest and you know what she saw? Twenty-five other Black Jesuses nailed on the cross and hung up on the walls." Marcy throws her head back tapping her teeth with the end of her paint brush. "But Amanda, the whole thing is not without irony because..." She leans towards me for effect. "The lady who won last year, Maria Munoz, she was a Mexican lady who painted the Savior as a Chinamen!" She slaps her wheelchair. "Can you believe it?"

I eye her cuckoo clock. "Weird."

She taps the thin wood against her teeth and mumbles, "A *Mexican* too. I mean, aren't all the Latinos devout Catholics?"

I shrug and wonder how many heart attacks would ensue if I spray painted on every carefully crafted picture, a big black cock on top of the withered and wasted loins of our Savoir on the cross. I keep staring at the clock waiting for that bird to pop out and shriek three o'clock.

"That's too bad for Teresa, I guess."

She takes the brush off her teeth and scowls, "Why?"

"Well... I mean she sort of *set the trend*, you know?"

"What?"

"Well, like, she set the trend and the next year everyone was doing and..." I laugh, slap the table, Marcy's eyes shoot to the paints. "Oh, come on, Marcy..."

"*What*?"

"She paints a black Jesus and gets booted, everyone else does the same thing the next year and then some Mexican wins with her Chinese Christ? Seems a tad unfair."

"How?"

I shake my head and roll my eyes, "Oh never mind."

She shrugs and fills a circle marked *nineteen* with Venetian red. "I don't see it."

"Whatever, when's this thing due anyway?"

"What?"

"This thing, the painting." I fan a hand in the direction of the Last Supper. "When's it due?"

"The entry date?"

"Yeah, that."

"Oh, not until June. I have the next two months to do it *perfect*."

I nod, get up, look in the fridge for a Coke. There's only rotten food and a bucket of compost housing dozens of writhing maggots. I turn around. "Marcy...what's this?"

Her shoulders slump a little, and she looks so old. "I can't go grocery shopping..."

"Well *yeah* but I thought we had that Danny boy come deliver for you. This isn't cool, you should have told me, I..."

"I don't *need* you to do every little thing for me, Amanda."

I look back in her fridge, maggots slipping in and out of broken egg shells. "Marcy... what've you been eating?"

She points with her paint brush at a pile of Chinese noodle boxes, Pizza boxes, Wings, Pasta shells dried and hardened fallen on the floor. "I call the restaurants when I need to."

"What!"

"I *have* to eat sometime!"

"Yeah but..."

"And it's not like *you've* been going to the grocery store lately. I should be asking *you* the same thing!"

"Well, I work a lot and go for dinner at friends' houses..." I think about the maggoty girl with the legs I axed wide open. I've been eating her for a month. The last time I was in a grocery store— about two weeks ago—was to buy some lettuce for the rat I sewed inside her stomach. I ate spaghetti and watched it claw its way out of her vagina. When he got out, the little fucker was racing around my living room, darting here and there. It took me forever to catch him. My intention was to see if I could keep him alive and strong enough to sew him in again, so I bought lettuce. Sadly though, this killed the poor little guy. "Marcy, eating out all the time is too expensive."

"Well it's not like *I* have many friends now, *is* it?"

"Marcy, I can cook for you."

She looks like she's about to cry, but she bats away the tears and her face turns hard. "I don't need you wiping my ass and spoon feeding me. You have other things to do, I'd just be holding you back. You'd be married by now, you know that." Her little stringy fist bangs the wheel of her chair. "*You* are the child, not *me*."

I close the fridge door and put my hand on her shoulder. "You are not a burden to me."

She freezes up, so I run my fingers through her hair, pat her on the back. She takes a deep breath then slowly relaxes. She pats my hand. "I know, dear. I just want you to live your own life."

"Marcy.... you *are* my life. Please, don't forget that." I try my best to mean this, but even as these words pass through my lips, and I can *feel* them warm her heart, I don't mean a word, because I'm wondering when she will die. My hand patting her shoulder, stroking her hair, I'm actually wondering if she's ever had an orgasm. I'm wondering if Jesus really was black, or Chinese, and I'm fighting the impulse to squeeze her shoulder, to see if I could break anything before she managed to make me stop, or if she *could* make me stop. "I love you, Marcy."

She sighs. "I know, love. I know."

I clean her fridge while she makes a grocery list. After I toss all the rotten apples and rancid meat in the trash, and throw the compost in the back yard, I go to Walgreens and buy all her food. The brunette bagging my groceries winks at me. She can't be a day over seventeen. I blush and then take Marcy's stuff home for her. I cook her spaghetti and help her get dressed for bed. We talk about plans for the trip to the Paint-by-numbers contest and she tells me all about men my age who attend.

"Some of them are real lookers. You really ought to come this year."

I nod, tuck in her blankets. "I know. I will."

I watch TV in her living room until the cuckoo clock announces ten o'clock. I turn off the TV and check if Marcy is asleep, then I drive back to Walgreens. I wait in the parking lot, listen to the radio and smoke cigarettes until that brunette grocery bagger girl comes walking out the door digging through her purse. As she gets closer she waves, I roll down the window, "Hey! What are you doing here?"

She laughs. "Umm, I work here?"

"Yeah but, until this hour? Don't you have homework?"

She laughs again. "Yeah, I do actually. Wait, what are *you* doing here?"

I point to the video store across the street. "Waiting for my friend to get off work."

"Oh. You know Dallas?"

I cough in my fist, looking around the parking lot. No one is here. "Yeah, that's my cousin."

"Oh cool! That's my boyfriend."

The best I can do to not frown is pull my face into a smirk. "Listen, you want a ride or something?"

She steps back, I could still hit her with the door before she broke into a run. "Well, I'm not really going far."

I point at the sky. "It's pretty dark, a lot of creeps out in the city tonight."

She doesn't say anything, so I start the engine. "I'm gonna go get Dallas some beer anyway, so if you just wanna come for the ride, I can take you back to him after."

Seventeen-year-old girls are so dumb. "Oh! Sure!"

We don't leave the parking lot. I undo my seat belt as she straps hers on. I swing a screwdriver straight into her windpipe, grab her hair and slam her head against the dash until I hear a loud crunch. I break the fingers she tries clawing me with and I light a smoke watching her as she slumps forward, her nose pouring like a bloody fountain onto the garbage bags on the seat and floor. When all that stops, I undo her seat belt and cover her with a blanket, then I drive home and cut up my groceries.

Chapter 20

Karl's friend Stephen, is getting married. Written vows, caged doves, real rings and everything.

Alison, she's hiking up the halter top of her dress, spitting in my ear, "Where we not supposed to wear white?"

Karl's friend Stephen is getting married to a woman he met online via a website for Ukrainian mail order brides.

Alison hisses in my ear so sharply I can *feel* the spit flying into my external auditory canal, beads of her saliva collecting on the bottoms of my hoop earrings. Her words, they are literally dripping onto my bare shoulder. "It's not like *she's* pure anyway. I'm not going to dress in slut colors just because *she* is parading around in faux virgin fabric. Look at her... she's probably been around the block a *hundred* times." It's kind of alarming how Alison crosses and uncrosses her legs when she says *virgin*.

Karl's friend Stephen, this chump hasn't even met his blushing bride. This wedding, the one I'm sitting at right now, hung over and dizzy, yeah this will be Stephen and whats-her-face's first time seeing each other, flesh wise. Alison points at the wrong woman. I wipe the beads of spit gathering on my earrings. "That isn't Sveta."

Alison looks over at some fat woman laced tight into an off-white bridesmaid dress and spooning borscht into the wide hole of her face. "Her?"

I shake my head. "Nope. That's just some bitch."

She keeps pulling up her halter top. "How do you know?"

"Because Stephen won't see her until she walks down the aisle."

"Really?"

"Yeah, really. Some people really *are* that lame."

Alison rolls her eyes, "*Traditional.*"

I shrug. "Lame."

She rolls her eyes again, quits pulling at her halter and crosses her arms and legs. "Well *I* don't think I'm wrong for wearing white if that pig over there gets to."

The borscht pig, the one in the white dress, she pops some pierogi in her mouth and smiles at some old man walking by. He doesn't smile back.

I poke Alison in the ribs, "Hey is my eyeliner smudged?"

She looks at me without smiling and shakes her head, "No sweetie, you look beautiful."

Karl sits down holding a napkin of Brie and Havarti squares. "Hey ladies."

Alison smiles, "Don't we look great? We got our hair and nails done this afternoon." She shakes her hands lose in front of her so Karl can see her manicured talons.

He pops a block of Havarti in his mouth. "Lovely!" He looks at my hair. "Wow! Amanda, I've never seen you with your hair up." He pops another piece of cheese in his mouth. "Beautiful."

I scratch my legs with my Mary Janes. These tights I'm wearing are itchy as hell, but I have to have them on or else everyone will ask me how I got that scar on the back of my leg. I got from the chick I killed, the one who popped me in the back of the knee with a pair of scissors. Yeah, I don't need to draw any more attention to these things. I was a little worried about going strapless because of the five claw marks on my right shoulder, but when the woman at the dress store saw them she asked if they were like that Khmer tattoo of Angelina Jolie's.

She said, "You know, the 'Know Your Rights' one." I was going to say no, Angelina's tattoo is on the other shoulder. I was going to say, no, these are scars are from a woman trying to save her own life. I was so tempted to say, I'm a murderer and it turns me on to rape, kill, and eat women. But instead I lied, "Yeah, 'Know Your Rights.' I'm a big fan of Jolie." I even nodded, grinned, and acted fun and everything. Though I got the feeling, even when I acted just right and didn't speak out of turn and bought all the shit she told me to, I got the feeling that bitch at the dress store knew I was rotten. When we waved goodbye from the car, I was so tempted to give her the finger and kill Alison and I both by driving through the wall of the bridal shop.

"Totally beautiful." Karl's cheeks are packed with so much Brie he's drooling wide strands of milky looking spit all over the front of his tuxedo.

Eventually the groom's side is stocked full, so Stephen asks half of everyone to sit on the bride's side. Karl, me, and Alison, we don't move a muscle. We're sitting in the back row in white picnic chairs. The only three people this far back on the groom's side. Everyone else on Stephen's side is up front. But it's ok because we look cool. We look like the bad kids.

Some old Ukrainian woman sings a song, completely flat and acapella. She's wailing away underneath a wreath of artificial flowers where the priest is waiting for the old pronouncing man and wife shtick, the worthless pay check and the free bar. This old woman, the one singing in Ukrainian, she goes on and on for a good eight minutes in this terrible language I would never want to understand *or* appreciate. I keep rolling down my evening gloves to check my watch.

Alison pokes my arm, "I thought no one here came from her country."

I can see the cheese being reduced to mush in Karl's mouth as he speaks, "Yeah, why are they all sitting on this groom's side?"

Alison rolls her eyes, "People will do the weirdest things to fit in."

Karl's mushy cheese breath blowing down my neck, "I don't understand *why* they had an *outdoor* wedding and we're sitting here under the goddamn *tents*. Why not just rent a hall or something? It'd be cheaper." He pops another block in his mouth, a drop of white spit plopping into his sleeve. "*And* easier to clean up."

The old man, the one who walked by the borscht bitch, the piggy one in the cheap dress who's now sitting on the grooms side, stuffing her face with Torte, yeah that old guy who didn't smile at her, well, he turns around now, frowns at us and puts a finger to his lips.

The priest says something to Stephen, he stands up, digs in his suit pocket for a second then nods to the priest. A fat bitch with a huge purple birth mark on her face springs off her chair, launching towards a tiny table holding a large portable CD player. It was hooked up to two giant wooden speakers that look so old and crumbly they would be reduced to dust at the slightest bump of bass. She presses play then retracts like a Jack-in-the-box, back into her front row seat on the bride's side.

Everyone turns around to see the bride come stepping slowly out from behind two large cream-colored drapes that part the very moment Madonna comes to life through those ugly speakers. I'm surprised because they actually sound pretty good. It reminds me of the saying 'don't judge a book by the cover.' I laughed because I wondered if that would play out as foreshadowing for this entire wedding. I decided to watch very closely.

"Life is a mystery...." I itch the scar on the back of my knee and smile as the bride steps into the aisle with Madonna singing, "I hear you call my name, and it feels like *home*..."

The bride, I've never met her. I know her name is Sveta. She's got the body of an anorexic teenage cheerleader, only hotter. I can't see her face, but I'm immediately disinterested when I see her hair is blonde, long and thick. I'm reminded of the waitress—what's her name—Kim. I remember her strapped into a chair, huffing beneath the saran wrap wrapped around her entire head.

I can't see Sveta's face because she's wearing that damn veil. I check my watch again, hoping the foreshadowing I mentioned earlier, happens soon.

Madonna whines, "I want you to take me there!" as Sveta approaches the priest. When she's face to veiled face with Michael, the woman with the birthmark on her face, she dashes forward, slapping the *stop* button. Everyone looks forward. You could hear a pin drop. I prayed for a fart.

Somewhere off in the distance a car honks twice and a dog starts barking. While Stephen reads his feelings off a flash card I can't stop staring at the perfect bow in Sveta's back, her perky tits and stick arms. Her figure is so perfect she looks like Leta Laroe came to life with a head of honey blonde hair curled against her back.

Alison whispers, "There are blondes in the Ukraine?"

I poke Karl, "Alison is retarded."

Pieces of wet cheese foaming at the corners of his lips growing into soppy streams of creamy spit, "I know."

I lean back to Alison, "Yes."

She shrugs and spits in my ear again, "That's *weird*."

When the bride says, "I do." And Stephen starts crying and everyone is blowing snot into hankies, Sveta lifts up her veil and they kiss. Karl leans into one ear, "Butter face."

I nod and whisper back. "Two out of ten."

I laugh because I just remembered God didn't answer my fart prayer for earlier, when the priest says, "May God be with you." Some old asshole, turns around again frowning at us. He puts his finger against his lips. I'd flip him the bird but Sveta is looking at me and I can feel little chunks of Karl's cheese rolling down the side of my face.

Fatty pushes play again, skipping to the beginning of *Like a Prayer* and the whole song starts over again. Only this time, thank God, everyone is getting up from their chairs and moving around, walking towards the bride and groom.

It's always a great relief when I speak without whispering, "Alison, give me a napkin."

She checks around her, "Don't got."

Karl is getting up, walking over to the buffet, I follow him when a napkin is suddenly right in front of me. I take it, wipe my ear which causes a bunch of makeup to come smeared off.

"Thanks, this..." I look up to see a girl so beautiful my heart skips a full beat and I have to close my eyes for a second to keep myself from passing out.

When I open them again, the girl is still there, an awkward grin on the whitest skin I've ever seen. Her hair is bright red, but not the gross kind of red. She's got eyes so stunning, so bright green I can't look at them directly when she asks "Are you okay?" Her words, all tumble from red bow lips, the most beautiful silk ribbons, the kind you would never untie.

"Hi." I go to shake her hand but the napkin, with all my makeup and mashed cheese hits the tiny palm of her perfect hand and I feel so dizzy I can't say anything except, "Great party..." before stumbling away. I sit outside, have a smoke and wait for Karl to come out of the tent dragging Alison with him.

He's laughing, spinning his keys around his finger as we walk to Alison's car. "So, I see you met Stephen's sister."

A passing breeze moves through my body, chilling me to the center of my bones. "Who was..."

He throws a thumb over his shoulder back towards the tent. "That red head. That's Stephen's older sister. She asked me if you were drunk."

I shake my head and fumble with opening the door, my whole face feels hot, my chest feels tight and heavy. "But I'm, I wasn't, I'm wasn't not..."

Karl is staring at me, Alison pauses at her door in the front. I can barely look up because my chest keeps getting tighter and tighter and it's getting harder and harder to breathe. "I'm *not* drunk!"

He squints, his voice getting real calm. "I know Amanda, it's okay."

I light another smoke and we pull away into traffic. Karl unwinds his window, lights a cigarette. "It's ok, Amanda, don't worry about it."

I flick the ash of my cigarette out the window. "I got some shit to do at home, drop me off, I'll call you guys later."

Alison turns on the radio, bobs her head to the rhythm of a song I don't know the name of, but have heard enough to hate. "But it's the wedding party!"

Karl laughs, "Shut the heck up! Since *when* do you give a *flip* about wedd'n parties?"

She turns the radio up higher, "Whatever, I just *do* okay?"

He shakes his head, "Yeah yeah, whatever."

At a traffic light I put my head between my knees, I hear Karl call from the driver's seat, "Amanda, you ok? You going to puke?"

I sit up, lean my head back and close my eyes, "No, my chest just is..."

Alison says, "Panic attack. It's okay, I used to get them all the time."

I open my eyes but everything is either too bright or too blurry so I close them again. "What the fuck is a panic attack?"

Karl reaches an arm back and snaps his finger in my face, I open my eyes, and he looks at me serious for a second then smiles, his eyes going back to the road. "I deal with them all the time at work. Well..." He shifts gears, " I mean *I* don't but a lot of the patients have them. Don't worry, you can't die from one, no matter how much you *feel* like you're really dying, you won't."

"What?"

He looks in his rear-view mirror, passes a minivan full of car seats and toddlers and shifts gears again. "You can't *die* from them."

"Oh."

"Yeah, so don't worry about it."

I scratch the scar on the back of my knee again, "Well, what the fuck?"

He checks his rear-view mirror and changes lanes. "What the fuck, *what*?"

I close my eyes, open them, light another cigarette and try cracking my neck. "Well what the fuck is this? What brings them on?"

Karl shrugs, "Nothing really. They can happen for no apparent reason. It's just the mind's way of coping with stress."

"Oh."

Alison turns the radio down. "Amanda, don't worry about it. I used to get them all the time."

I tap the ash off my cigarette. "What made them go away?"

She's quiet for a second staring out the window, "I don't know. They just sort of went away."

As we're driving down the bare road to my house at the very end of the street Karl says, "I'm sure Stephen didn't even notice, and his sister is cool. I know her from work."

I nod, check the time under my glove. "What's her name?"

He stops the car in front of my house and spins the dial through a dozen or so radio stations as I undo my seatbelt. "Sophia."

Sims

Chapter 21

Sinners Circle

After work on Monday, I come home and read President Clinton's commemoration statement about the deportation and massacre of one and a half million Armenian people.

The next day, *M*A*S*H* is just starting when Clinton comes back on through breaking news. He says two students went into their high school and started shooting before turning the guns on themselves. He quotes Saint Paul. "We see through a glass darkly." He says we need to teach our children to express their anger. He says we have to watch for early warning signs. President Clinton tells everyone to pray for Littleton. Then he talks about God.

I turn off the TV and sit there for a minute. I move to the window and watch an old man riding a bicycle down the street.

I put my jacket on and walk to the park with my hands in my pockets. It's raining. I spend the rest of the afternoon tearing the wings and legs off insects running for cover.

Everything always runs away when it's time to go. Everything is cowardly and childish. Even the old. I bet death could live for eternity on the days begged from every man.

I kill the bugs. I kill all of them. None of them get away.

Does this make me a *bad guy*?

Because, I spear for glory and wipe out the weak? Isn't this how human beings evolved? The strong are dangerous because the weak cause us to be. Too bureaucratic. If a wolf is bothered by another wolf, he attacks it. One wolf lives, one wolf dies.

This is nature. I will not be put under the thumb of a weak, pudding bellied man simply because he fails to act on his evolutionary instinct. No warden.

If they can't catch me, then they are dumb and I am not. Therefore, I am free to unravel deep inside my own Disneyland. Where everything is Christmas and smells like girls.

Mom is upstairs and we're having dinner at five thirty. The love of my life is laying in my lap, touching my face on a sunny afternoon. She's smiling and I'm so happy.

Somewhere a bird is singing, and my heart is breaking. I shut my eyes and sing softly to myself. *"I'm in the park."* I shake my head. I open my eyes. I'm in the park.

A car alarm goes off, sounding near my house. I get up, brush myself off, blow under my nails and walk back to my house, completely relaxed.

I'm feeling the soft air flutter through my eyelashes and tickle my cheeks. I pray an angel-from-heaven kind of girl has broken down in front of my house and gets horny while waiting for the tow truck and she sucks on my clit gentle, then firm. Her mouth totally loving, totally mine.

I smile as I walk onto the road in front of my house. And would you believe it? It wasn't an angel-from-heaven at all. In fact, it was that stupid old man riding by on a bicycle earlier. Yeah, and here he is now, across the street from me, shutting off his car alarm. He's got the trunk popped on a station wagon fixed up with all the bells and whistles.

What a dickhead.

Hands in pockets, I walk toward my house. He's looking at me like he wants to ask me something. I don't want to help him.

But as I'm directly across the street he shouts, "Miss! Excuse me?"

I stop walking and smile, using my hand to shield my eyes from the sun. "Yes?"

He hesitates, he doesn't know if he should shout and is waiting to see if I will walk over to him. That is a display of submission. I stand there smiling.

He takes a step closer, then a few more. His demeanor is weak and cowardly. He's probably entitled and has sexual hang ups. White moustache, white hair, blue polo shirt tucked into white pants. He looks like Ned Flanders saw a ghost.

He says to me, "Pardon me miss but, I'm responding to a news-paper advertisement..." Holy shit. This guy. "...orchard picked apples for sale. What I'd really like to do, Miss, is figure out which of these houses he is in. I left the darn address at home and..."

He is standing between two parked cars on the street. I am in front of him. Behind him, a vehicle passes and for a brief moment, is completely trapped. His smile is easy, his eyes wide and honest. He doesn't even realize what he's done.

I take a step forward and laugh, short electric shocks snap through my entire body, as black waves of cum and Christmas wash over me in megacosm. Ce que j'ai fait, ce soir la.

As a truck passes behind him, I take a step forward. I say, "Well... sir, I'll tell you what *I'd* really like to do. I'd really like to warn you that there are some *real* weird people around here. *Real* weird. Yup, and they look totally normal, just like you and me."

He's confused. Another car passes behind him and I move until I'm far enough away that I'm exactly out reach.

I appear totally normal and definitely attractive as I continue. "Really creepy fucking people, okay? And some of those weirdos want to take you over there into my house. And then they're not even gonna wait. They're just gonna start pulling all your teeth out and putting them back in different spots, right in the kitchen! They're gonna fuck'n hit you in the dick tip with an icepick! Catch ya in the ass crack with an axe that used to attack whoever touched it last! Haunted shit. Ghost stories, okay? Then they'll snap your jaw wide open with a vice and use it as a how-to guide for when they do it to your wife, when she comes looking for you!"

His face is totally white, his pupils look like a cartoon. I calmly turn and walk into my house. Once I'm inside, I can't stop laughing. Even in the shower. I run up the stairs to Marcy's floor to see how she's doing. If she

Sims

asks me why I'm laughing, I'm tell her I saw something funny on TV. I'll say I was watching, The Simpsons.

But when I get up there she's in the kitchen on the phone and holds a finger up at me to be quiet for a moment. The fluorescent bulb above her shitty dinner table, always gives me the creeps. It reminds me of poverty and nights at home without mom, listening to the sound of rain on the roof of our trailer. I hated Marcy's table too, it reminded me of mornings when mom was grumpy or too busy to have breakfast with me.

I sit in the recliner in front of the TV. There is too much orange in this room. Orange makes me feel isolated and alone. I can hear the clock and it's breaking my heart. Suddenly the fear of falling asleep and remaining in this orange room forever, fills me with horror. I close my eyes and imagine that Hell is a frozen tundra where the doomed must freeze forever inside eternity. Our mouths howling in slow motion, time suspended, we are slowly screaming forever. Until everything is nothing and we are gone and none of this ever happened. Nothing really matters. I am in this chair, in this room, frozen in hell.

I open my eyes again and stand up. I brush my hair back out of my face and watch Marcy hang up the phone. She looks me dead in the face and says, "That was, Paul Merry! From down the street! He says someone looking for his house to buy apples was threatened by a crazy homeless woman!"

I remember a victim of mine once, she made the sincerest expression of total innocence on her face. I was so impressed with it, that after I killed her, I spent a very long time in front of the mirror working on it. I think I'm pretty good at it. If I wasn't me, and I was talking to me, I would believe me. So, I make the face and I say to Marcy, "Oh no! Call the police!"

Marcy shakes her head and shrugs, "Well, you think he would." She sighs and rolls her wheelchair toward the bedroom, mumbling. "People always leave the problem for someone else."

Sinners Circle

Chapter 22

The sun in this room, it will pull your heart apart. The glare on the window, the transparent me staring back at the mortal me, in real time. It makes me want to die. I can't move away from the side of this empty bed no matter how much my thighs shake and tremble. My mind won't take me away from staring back at myself in the glass, my spirit self in an empty room of unhooked breathing machines and clean bed sheets pulled tight at the corners.

I put my hand on my arm, looking at the empty bed in the reflection of the glass and gasp when my fingers meet each other and my cheeks burn from salty beads slipping down the sides my face, into the corners of my mouth and drip onto the numb scars on my chin.

I bite my tongue and feel the same strikes shredding all the way down my heart, the same stinging I felt when I slid down the walls of my foster home when I was young and mom was printed in halftone all over the newspaper.

My gaze never leaves the panes of glass burning my eyes blind with sun light, even when I trace the polished surface of the bedside table with my fingertips. The bare table that never changed the whole time Lilly was in that bed remains flowerless, undecorated, as it always was, dustless and blank.

I close my eyes and feel the fleshy burden of my wet lids closing together. I remember her.

When we're finished smoking against the brick of the building at work, I kiss her forehead, ears eyes and mouth. I zip up her little red leather jacket. I tell her to have fun and I pat her on the ass as she dissolves into nothing and is gone.

I open my eyes, wipe the tears from my cheeks, and lay a pair of pussy willows down onto the pillow. I don't look back in the window, I just fold my arms and leave the hospital with little Lilly's words winnowing through the cavities of my heart.

Chapter 23

"What's the best part about raping a two-year old?" Blaine is in his office, shouting into a telephone I doubt is even plugged in. The customer at my counter, the one fishing in his pockets for eighteen cents, he looks embarrassed. Blaine's feet slap the floor so frantically it sounds like he's being strangled from behind. "Feeling her hip bone snap!"

I slip the customers issue of *Leg Show* magazine in a bag and smile as he walks out of the store all sunken and depraved.

"What has seventeen nipples, is black and stinks?" His feet slap the floor again like he's choking to death. "A garbage bag outside a breast cancer clinc!"

For me, the worst thing about this whole phony phone conversation business isn't the fact it's extremely disturbing to the psyche that he would go on and on about awful things to himself while pretending he was communicating with another human being because that's *fine* by me. No, what makes it so goddamn awful is he's so fuckin' bad at it. He doesn't pause properly in between sentences the way you actually would while the person on the other end of the conversation is responding to your comments. Blaine just keeps yakking away like a maniac. The way he's going on and on, you don't even need to see the phone cord is unplugged to figure out he's only talking to himself.

That scuffing of his feet shambling the slick cement floor of his janitor closet office comes fulminating through his tiny space into the front of the store. His tone changes, slow and drawling. "Hey did you know that *Jonbenet Ramsey* is an anagram for 'Enjoy semen, brat'!"

I check my watch; my shift was over five minutes ago. I walk to the back, grab my jacket off the rack and almost run Karl over in the alley while lighting a cigarette as I pull my car out. "Amanda!"

I roll down my window and tap the ash onto the ground. "What?"

He walks around the side and slides into the passenger's seat. "Wanna give me a ride?"

I tap my smoke out the window again. "Sure."

When we're out on the highway he points down the street I wasn't going to take. "Down here."

I drive for a few blocks while he fumbles with the radio and lights one of my cigarettes. "Where are you going?"

He blows smoke through a pair of grinning lips. "What? Do you mean 'where are *we* going'?"

I stop at a traffic light, a twelve-year-old girl and her fat mother are lip syncing to some terrible song in the mini can next to me. I drop my cigarette out onto the street and roll up my window. "Huh?"

Karl shakes his head. "Well your house first, I guess."

"What the fuck?"

His knuckles tapping his knees, he turns up the radio and air drums on the dashboard. "What the fuck, what?"

I just stare at him. The light turns green and I shrug. "Where are you going?"

He covers his eyes with his whole hand and laughs. "The *dance* dummy!"

"What dance?"

He turns the radio down. "The dance I told you about last week at work."

"You told me about what? Dude, you didn't say shit about some dance or whatever."

"What the fuck? Yeah, I did. I brought you coffee and everything. You were all zoned out, I had to drop the goddamn cup in front of you and say 'drink' to get your attention. Weren't you listening?"

"Oh."

"What?"

"No, I said 'Oh' not 'No.'"

"Oh."

"Yeah."

"So, you remember?"

"No."

"What?"

I light a cigarette. "I mean yeah I remember you brought coffee I just, I dunno, must've forgot."

"Well no one really remembers coffee I guess."

"No, I remember that, I just don't remember the dance part."

"Oh."

"Yeah."

He scratches his chin and rolls down his window a bit. "So what's up?"

"Oh, I dunno. Nothing I guess."

"No, I mean, are you coming or what?"

"To the dance?"

"Yeah"

"Oh."

He points towards the direction of my house. "Just turn up here."

"What's with all these direction and shit? I know the way to my own house."

He sighs and steals another one of my cigarettes. "Whatever."

When we get to my house I shave my legs in the shower, put some vitamin lotion on my scars and throw on a tank top and jeans. I'd wear my shell shoes but their crusted with blood. Karl claps two VHS tapes together while I'm lacing up my Converse high tops and says, "Why do all these tapes have hair glued to them?"

I finish tying my shoes, walk over and snatch them away from him. "Don't touch my shit."

He shakes his head and says, "Bring a coat."

I grab my favorite black hoodie, and we drive until we're in the parking lot of the hospital. "Uh, what kind of dance is this?"

"Staff."

"Why isn't Alison here?"

"Because she doesn't work here."

"Then why am *I* here?"

"Because Sophie is here."

"She works here?"

"Coma ward. Yeah."

"But *I* don't work here."

"It's okay."

"If it's okay for me to be here then why didn't Alison come?"

He shrugs, put his hand on the door handle. "Because she doesn't work here."

Being led through all these side entrances and 'STAFF ONLY' areas, staring at the back of your friends' head, it's like a bad dream you are inwardly panicking to wake from. The only thing worse than having a nightmare that resembles this sort of chaos is the horror that it is actually happening and unlike a dream you can't wake up and make it go away. All your conversations have listeners and all your actions have real consequences.

Sims

After following Karl up a hundred stairs and down a thousand staff corridors we arrive in the psych ward common area, through a door I never noticed before.

Inside this big room, I have to open and close my eyes to make sure I'm not dreaming, or off in some field screaming and crying, high on copious amounts of LSD. The whole place is decorated, *transformed* into a disco ball dangling play pen for loonies. All sorts of banners are hung up across the walls. *Happy Easter* over the punch bowl, *It's a BOY!* by the medicine window. *Merry Christmas* and *Happy Birthday* hanging over the DJ switching CD's, while committed men and women wearing pajama pants and felt slippers sip anxiously at the red contents of their tiny Dixie cups.

Karl points at a *Get Well Soon* banner by the couch I always read Cherry Blossom on. "Patients decorated most of it."

I nod and scan the room for Sophie but I don't see her anywhere, there's too many people walking around, bumping into one another and mumbling to themselves. "Oh."

"Yeah it was sort of an activity for them for the past couple days. Motivation exercise."

"Oh."

I follow him to the punch bowl. The King of France is there his little wash cloth cape still pinned to the back of his shirt. He sees me and walks away, his eyes full of tears. Karl smiles at a woman standing over the juice. "Hi Linda."

She smiles and pours us both cups. He raises his cup to her, "Cheers." We walk over to some corner of the room, him waving at people every two seconds, asking how they are.

I stare into the red juice, swirl it around in the cup and wonder if this some kind of mass suicide plan. A way to thin out the load of crazies. "So, what's the occasion?"

He waves at a girl who looks like she hasn't bathed in weeks. "Hi

Caitlyn!"

I'm filled with horror when she smiles back and her teeth and lips are stained red, I look at Karl as he lowers his Dixie, and he looks like he's just chewed through his own leg. The more I glance around the room, the more I see that almost every single person—staff or patient, it doesn't matter— they all look like vexed cannibals bobbing their heads to nineties hits.

I walk over to the trash bin and drop my cup in. Bright rays of white light burn into my eyes blinding me as I walk back to where Karl and I were standing, but he's not there anymore and neither is Caitlyn, and a man twisting his t-shirt into a fabric handle is laughing at his hands and smiling at me with all that red punch stained to his teeth. Two fat men eating Nanaimo bars off napkins push past me. I stand on my tippy toes looking for that door Karl and I came through when Madonna's *Like a Prayer* comes on.

I can feel the hair on the back of my neck stand up, my skin getting warmer as a few people by the DJ start swaying to the words. There's an approaching sensation I can't shake, but I'm not afraid because the stronger it gets, the more calm I feel.

I close my eyes and relax my hands. My mind is still and my heart is tepid as Madonna's words float through me. "I hear you call my name...and it feels like *home*..."

Something warm and smooth touches my fingertips. I open my eyes to see Sophie standing in front of me her ribbon bow lips parted into a grin. She is the only person in the room without a juice stain. "Amanda?"

"Hi."

She blushes, looks down at her shoes, then back into my face. "Hi, I'm Sophie."

All that terrible light that was blinding me, but right now as she stands in front of it, if angels were real, they would look just like her. I'm not sure if they are supposed to have red hair though. I wouldn't know, I've never seen one, but during my twenty-seven years in this world I can say that without a doubt Sophie is the most beautiful woman I have ever laid eyes on.

"Hi, Sophie."

"Would you like some punch?"

"No."

She laughs, and my snatch gets wet so fast I almost have an orgasm when she touches my shoulder. "Oh good. Me neither." She pushes a finger through her lips, takes it out of her mouth and looks at it. I have a sharp and sudden desire to be inside of her body. My skull throbs with vibration as the Witch Drums break into my mind, beat into my thoughts. My clit is rock hard and my vagina is crawling like a caterpillar when Sophie smiles at me again. I lean into the edge of the table, like I'm reaching for something to eat. I press my clit into the table and mumble quietly mid-orgasm.

The crazies all around me, dancing under the *Happy Anniversary* banners, the plastic *Welcome Home* pennons, all these lunatics with their faces dyed red, teeth turning them all into vampires and Sophie smiling in front of me, I laugh so hard that I start crying.

She puts her hand on my shoulder, pinches my arm. I'm smiling, wiping tears out of my eyes and trying to keep my voice from cracking when she says, "Are you okay? Are you okay?"

I have to step back, catch my breath; the room's tilting left then right, it starts spinning, my heart swelling huge every time Sophie takes a step closer and touches me. The more I blink, the more my vision blurs and I'm wiping my face so fast I don't notice everything go black until I'm on my back laying on the floor. Before I know I'm even sprawled out here, Sophie's head is on my chest, the music is off and all the juice drinking cannibals are staring at me. They look bored. I sit up, my hand grabbing Karl's shoe. He kneels down. "You okay?"

I nod, but I'm so dizzy I almost fall back down, Sophie catches my head. "You passed out. Do you want us to call a doctor?"

I shake my head. "No, I'm fine. I just... need some air."

Sophie looks at Karl, Karl looks at Sophie, Sophie looks at me. "Would you like to go home?"

I fish in my pocket, hand Karl my keys. He looks at Sophie. "I have to watch the floor until ten."

She frowns. "Are you working shift?"

He nods, tucks my keys in his pocket. "Yeah..." He helps me to my feet. All the nearby nut cases give me dirty looks.

Linda from the punch bowl pushes a cup in my hand, even though its water, I still swirl it around before gulping it down. Sophie takes it away from me, crushes it and puts it in her pocket and sighs. "I guess, I mean, I can take her home."

Karl pats my shoulder. "She lives way on the other side..."

The music starts back up and I'm about to tell them I'm fine, I'm completely okay, but Sophie says, "No I mean back to my place. She can crash on the couch." I shut my mouth, put a hand to my head like I'm still dizzy and just stand there waiting.

This time, on the way down to the parking lot, we take the elevator and leave through the main doors.

Steering through traffic she tells me all about her pet cat. At a traffic light she tells me how much she doesn't like dogs. At a four way stop she says, "My favorite smell ever is, you know when you huff on a sleepy kitten stretching and just waking up? Or a hamster that's sound asleep? That's my favorite ever."

Her whole apartment smells like fresh cucumbers and she even fluffs the pillow on the bed she made for me on the couch. Later, when I'm lying there staring at her spotless ceiling listening to her hum as she cuts up a lemon to put in some ice water for me, she tells me that the bathroom is down the hall if I need it, right beside her bedroom. When she disappears for a few minutes and then comes back in her pajamas, she wishes me good night and closes her door. I wait a few minutes.

    I pull down the covers she tucked around me and I sneak quietly to her bedroom. I close my eyes and think of her head on my chest and her hand on my shoulder. I think about how wet I got when she touched my shoulder. I think about her hands and fingers looped through mine in the elevator. When I open my eyes again, my hand is on the center of her bedroom door. I sigh, taking my hand away, to sway at my side. I walk back to the couch and crawl back under the blankets. As I sleep I dream about my mother humming to me and playing with my hair while she drank gin and we watched TV. I dream about Gina in the bathtub. I dream about lemons and cucumbers, cats and traffic lights. I dream of Sophie and angel wings. I dream of maggots, bullets and broken glass. I dream of two dead deer on my front lawn. And then I am awake and Sophie is holding out a mug of Chamomile tea for me. She smiles and asks, "How was your sleep?"

Chapter 24

Fast forward to three weeks later. I hadn't gotten laid or even masturbated. Absolutely nothing happened. I went to work, I came home, went into the basement and bounced a ball off the wall beside the body.

It wasn't much of a corpse. More like a pile of slime and maggots. Dirt and Yellow Bones. I liked it though. I felt like I had someone there to talk to when my mind gets so bungled up I start shouting. But at the same time, I felt alone and I hated it.

I needed something else other than sex. I don't know why but, I'd been pretty emotional lately. Sometimes, I numb out for long periods of time and then without warning, I'll have this huge emotional crash.

But, today was okay. Even though the sun is setting, that's what I tell myself anyway. Just to keep higher spirits.

I'm just getting off work and walking through the alley to my car. I jiggle the keys and run a hand through my hair. It's soft, long and thick. Sometimes I wish I had a girlfriend that would play with my hair.

I smile as I get in and shut the door. I start the engine and pull off into an alley I rarely take. Just to keep things new.

Sometimes I wish I'd get caught. But escape. Then I could leave the country and just leave this life behind. I could feel sand under my feet.

Ocean waves washing across my face. Long French grass on my fingertips.

I would like to live on a beach. In a cave. I could live somewhere just outside a tiny village of loving, trusting people. People who thought nothing of sending their daughters off down a long road by the ocean. Totally alone.

Yes, I would live in paradise, in a cave, watching the town from a distance and when a young woman was to be married, I would scoop her away from her house or murder her lover and then carry her to my cave through some kind of tunnel system. And I could keep her alive because no one would hear her scream and I could crush her into mush and cram her entire body inside of me. And I'd die because of it.

I was coming to a light when I sneezed, my body lurching forward. My forehead hit the horn, I felt a thump under the back wheels and laughed as a uni-cycle flew into the air. I checked all my mirrors, nobody saw. I chuckled to myself again.

I slowed down then re-checked my mirrors. I licked my lips and backed up. Laying on the side of the road was a pile of dog shit next to a pile of rags. I slammed on the breaks and bolted out the door. At first, I heard the sound of the door beeping that it was open, but then the pounding of Witch Drums overtook me.

I marched over to the pile of shit. It reeked. I grabbed as much as I could, held my shirt out to carry more. I walked back to my car, dumped the shit in there. Then, I heard screaming, I looked further down the road, past the dog shit. There was a man with a bicycle helmet on, in spandex bicycle gear, spinning himself around, howling, screaming and waving broken arms like he's on an island signaling for rescue.

I laugh because I can't believe this happened. What are the odds? I keep laughing as I walk to him. The closer I get, the quieter he gets. I don't do anything. I just watch him.

My hands are in my pockets, I nod in observation. I'm a bit of a scientist you see? I'm not a complete monster. I'm not gonna just run him over and then come beat his brains out or anything. That would be a terrible thing to do to somebody! I laugh at the thought of it and bend forward.

I watch him roll over onto his back, his body is thrashing, he's screaming but I can't hear a sound. I watch him turn over and around, I watch the sunlight play across blood puddles. Some are darker than others. Cells die really, really fast. I close my eyes and meditate with that thought for a moment. When I open my eyes again, my heart is pounding in my ears. I wait for the Witch Drums.

Remember that road I was telling you about? The one I always wanted to hit someone on? Dreams come true. Wish bigger.

His lips move but I can't hear what he's saying. I feel his head for a fever and hum *Pink Floyd.*

He isn't bleeding anywhere except his face and nose. The shin bones are poking through the skin on both legs. That is called an open fracture. However, I can see, plain as day, and trust me, I'm no doctor but he's got compound fractures all over the place.

Just to be safe I carefully raise his arms above his heart.

He looks like someone's asshole dad who thinks golf if great. He's in pretty good shape though and I peg him at around thirty-five.

I reach to touch him, but he pulls away, smacking the back of his head on the pavement. I run my hands through his hair. He's got a little bit of salt and pepper coming through. I'm not brute force crazy about the rules when it comes to hair color going grey at a certain age, like during your thirties. Losing the color in your hair is hereditary, well, all hair issues are hereditary... wouldn't you think?

Once I skimmed through a magazine in a doctor's office, it was all about men's hair. It wasn't interesting.

I like his shoes. They're nice but, I wouldn't wear them.

I drag him by the feet into the back of my Jeep. Just before shutting the trunk, I take his shoes off and throw them in the tall grass of the field we're next to. I close and lock it before turning back around to check out the pile of rags. And bless the angels, for it was not a pile of rags at all. Rather two cats and mouse. I carried them back to my car, skipping to the backseat. I toss them in then climb into the driver's seat and burn down the highway clocking a cool seventy.

Sunrise was still with us and could be expected to remain so for the next half hour. I turn around to face the man as I peel the vehicle back up roads that lead to nowhere. The drive was bumpy and made my voice wobble as I told the guy, "Sunrise is still with us!"

He starts screaming and pounding the back of my seat. I press myself into his punches. I feel the wheels bounce beneath me, I think of my mom, rocking me to sleep.

The sun is setting, and the days final light is quickly fading. I drive into the center of a field, get out and open the back. I had laid the back seat down a few days ago when planning a road trip to Canada. I wanted to see how much space was in here, should I ever have to live in here for a while.

I pull him out by the shoulders of his jacket and dump him on grass I didn't expect to be wet. I use my arm and swept all the dog shit out. It was crusty and didn't stink bad, hardly stunk at all actually. I shut the back and turned around. The guy was covered in dog shit. I laughed, my hands covering my mouth, *"Oh my god!* I'm so sorry!" Then I kick him as hard as I could, across the face.

I walk to the back seat again, open the door and grab the two cats. I don't shut the door. I let the beep happen, I let the red-light in. I open the trunk. I close the trunk. I close all the doors. Then I drag this poor bastard to the grass in front of the Jeep. I slowly move back to the driver's seat, I rev the motor then hit the headlights. My cunt is squirming again. I want to laugh but my entire body is rattling with cum. My teeth are watering, my tits are hard. I rev the motor again then kill the engine. I leave the headlights on and get out and shut the door. I grab the two cats then walk

Sinners Circle

to where I'm just outside of the light but he can still see me.

He looks terrified, and honestly, his legs don't even look that bad anymore. A little swollen yeah, totally sure they're terribly broken for sure, but I guess what I'm really saying is, he's toughing it out. And I'm proud of him for that. Good job buddy.

I take off my clothes and spread my legs. I lift the cat up to my mouth, dangled by its tail in one hand, and with the other I crush the skull until it's head is goop.

I watch the guy, with one free hand I start tapping on my clit. His face is clammy, he has the eyes of a rich man. I open my mouth and drop the cat up to its belly, down my throat. I gag but, I know a trick with my throat muscles. It's like snake muscles. I don't know why but, I have an incredible amount of control with my throat muscles. I can swallow just about anything. Entirely.

Or at least I like to think I can. A lot of performers die from too much confidence. They take their eye off the ball, you see? Or is it the pressure of the crowd that drives one to be reckless? To act recklessly. Could wanting to excel in the eyes of your peers, could that not be categorized as aspects of the human condition though? Like Icarus. But, does this mean Man is conditioned to fail?

I swallow the cat up to its hips then push everything down. I have two bottles of water in the Jeep. I'm choking on hair, gagging on dead skin and slimy entrails. I've got pounds of rotten carcass inside me. Completely polluted. It feels disgusting. My clit is on fire. My whole-body burns. The cunt between my legs is pounding, throbbing and dripping sloppy wet. I step into the headlights so he can see me reach down my throat and regurgitate the cat. I cough and spit and laugh and spit and cough and then spit some more.

I lean over the guy. He's kind of a bummer actually. He hasn't done much of anything apart from lay there moaning and groaning and acting like he's five. He does pay attention pretty well though. I'll give him that. I make myself puke. I force myself. I shove fingers down my throat and wretch myself raw. All over his legs. At the end, I spit up at maggot and dig two out of my mouth.

The guy with the Rich Man eyes doesn't look rich anymore. He looks pale, broken and terrified.

I tap his shoulder. "You wanna fuck?"

I'm surprised he's even conscious. Must be adrenaline. Maybe he's in shock. Ah, right that must be it.

I laugh and give him a little kick. "Hey, you ready to get out of here? I'll take you to a hospital. You're gonna be just fine."

Even though I can clearly see that indeed, yes, he is definitely in shock, I can *still* tell that deep down, way down there, right down to the part of him that's still clinging on for hope and trying to live through this whole crazy thing, he is deeply relieved.

I smile, pat him on the shoulder then get back in my car. I kill the lights then get back out, grab all my clothes, then get back in the truck. When I turn the headlights back on and start the Jeep, I see there's a few pieces of clothes I'd missed. So, I get back out and pick those up too.

The sun is gone. I pull on my clothes then get lean over the guy as I'm wrestling on a sneaker. I say, "Can you walk?" I laugh "Sorry, that was mean. Hold on. I'll get you to a hospital, just hang on.

I get back in the Jeep, blast the high beams and rev the engine. I drive over the guy as he's trying to sit himself up.

I drive the speed limit all the way home.

Chapter 25

"He wrote me a love poem and then put it on my pillow. So, when I woke up this morning, even though he wasn't there, I could feel his love for me." Alison hugs a piece of paper to her chest. "I'm keeping this forever."

I crack my neck, tap my cigarette. "Whatever."

She closes her eyes and sighs. "How could you say something like that about something as beautiful as this?" She presses the paper deep between her tits.

I shake my head. "Love poems are the receipt, the proof of purchase, of all the crap you just bought into."

"What kind of sick person looks at love that way?"

I poke her paper chest. "Same question."

She frowns, turns around and goes back into the coffee shop. Trisha looks at me, but the second our eyes connect she drops her head and pretends to be cleaning a table.

I walk back to work. Blaine's sucking on something, probably a big wad of gum. "You got the inventory sheets done?"

I nod. "Yeah."

He sucks on that huge ball in his mouth. "Put them in my office when you got a minute."

"Sure." I grab the clipboard, flip through the sheets to make sure they are all there and hand it to him.

He keeps sucking, biting down and popping his jaw wide open between chews. "No, in my office."

I walk to his closet office but the door is locked, he stares at me for a few seconds, digs in his pockets and clears his throat while he sorts through a clinking mess of key rings. He tries a few but none work, eventually when one does and the door opens, I toss the clipboard onto his desk. A stress ball rolls off a pile of papers, falls and knocks over the garbage can, litter spilling all over the floor. Strangely though, the only trash in there is little balls of electrical tape and crunched up strips of paper. Blaine points to the corner at the end of the hall outside his office. There's a broom and dustpan leaning against the door frame of the bathroom. I sweep up his tape and paper trash, dump it all back into the bin and check my watch. My shift is over in ten minutes.

Blaine says, "Next week I'm not gonna be here for two days. So, I'll need you to do tills and closing on both nights."

"Sure."

He nods, turning that ball of rubber gum over in his mouth. "Okay good."

I stop for a pack of smokes and a case of beer at a convenience store.

When I get home, Sophie is sitting on my front steps reading a book. When I get out of the car and wave to her she doesn't stand up. She just sits there smiling and squinting the sun out of her eyes. "Oh good, you got your car back."

"Yeah Karl brought it back the other day after work."

She looks back at her book, shrugs, then back at me. "Well that's good, I guess."

"Yeah. What are you doing here?"

"Huh?"

I point to the house. "At my house. How'd you know I live here?"

She turns around, looks at the house, back at me and holds the book up to shield her eyes. I see the title. *Beauty and the Beast*. I stand in front of her so I block the sun. She laughs. "Oh, Karl dropped me off here after work today. I hope you don't mind."

I stop moving and stand totally still with cat-like readiness. "Why are you here?"

She blushes, looks down at her feet. "Karl… told me a few things and well, I thought maybe you would like to tell me a few things because…" Sophie, that beautiful girl, that woman with the glowing eyes that make my chest feel weak, she stands up and wraps her arms around me. Her hair smells like lilacs. "I want to tell you a few things." She backs up a little, "Do you think it's weird if I hug you?"

My head is swimming.

She looks down at her feet again. She doesn't say anything and I don't say anything and the silence keeps growing heavier with every second we don't say or do anything. I swing the case of beer a little. "I gotta go put this inside."

Well, at least that's what I meant to say. I felt like I was coming into the world through some kind of new birth. That's how it felt while she was kissing me. I couldn't believe it. My eyes squeezed shut, tears spilling down the side of my face and then I heard a shatter. Then a bottle being kicked away. Sophie stopped kissing me and I felt like I'd just been unplugged from paradise. My eyes wide, staring at this red-haired angel with long eyelashes and big green eyes like turtle shells. She was smiling, she ran a hand through her hair and I felt an ache, pang through my body. I wanted her to touch me. She kicked another bottle away, "Sorry…"

I was rapidly tumbling down the rabbit hole, I was madly in love with her.

I couldn't believe my luck. Sophie. Right here on my doorstep. I felt a vein in my chest warm for Karl. It curled around my rib cage once then was gone.

I smiled at Sophie. "Do you want to come inside?"

She blushes. "Sure." She is so beautiful.

As we're walking up the steps I reach in my pocket and get out my keys. I unlock the door then turn around "Hey can you hold this for a second?"

I hold out my hand like I'm going to give her something but instead I slip my fingers through hers so we're holding hands. She's surprised for a moment then squeals and slaps my arm "Oh my *god*! You!" And then she kisses me some more and I am in heaven. I feel gentle swoons move through my body, shaking my knees, draining all the blood from my face. I wrap my arms around her and we move to the couch. We're seamless and out of words. We're a pair of soft bodies and wet lips. Long hair and hard nipples. I lean in to lay on top of her and suck on her honey lips for eternity but, she sits up, puts her hands on my tits and pushes me back.

She says, "Don't you want to know what Karl told me?"

Oh right, Karl. I shake my head no but my mouth says, "Sure."

"Well, we work together."

"Oh, right."

"He told me what happened at the wedding and I thought that was really beautiful. I mean, I know what it's like to have social anxiety. I had it all throughout high school and college. I almost dropped out! Twice..."

Her lips looked like fat little cherries. Like a plum cut in half. A fat little plum. Her face was slender and porcelain.

I watch her mouth closely as she continues, "...I thought you were beautiful. I even told my cousin I thought you were sexy."

I'm lost in her eyes. She says, "I thought maybe you thought I was weird or something because of the way you acted at the dance."

I shake my head again, "No. You're amazing. I... I still can't believe this is even happening."

She smiles, leans in and kisses me. "I like you. I want to get to know you."

I think my favorite part about being a lesbian is how instantaneous and passionate love is. It's like two little bombs going off, one right after the other.

We put on pajamas and order Chinese. I even make sure they got all her stuff right. Because they always get mine so wrong all the time and I hate it.

We decided on *While You Were Sleeping* but, spent the whole-time kissing.

She said she wanted to sleep over and I made this silly ruse that I was going to make her a bed on the couch because I didn't want her to feel uncomfortable sleeping in my bed. But she laughed and then I ate her pussy for an hour. I didn't want to let her go down on me because, I felt worried all the maggots would have left a bad smell or something. But, I still couldn't believe this whole thing and I wanted to push my luck. So, I let her, and it was great! She didn't say anything and I watched her do it the entire time and she didn't make a weird face, like she was choking on or even tasting something wrong. This made me feel good.

Later that night when I got up to go pee, I was coming back from the bathroom and I watched Sophie sleep. She looked like an angel at ease. My heart felt light as candy floss. I slipped into bed next to her, kissed the crown of her head and whispered to no one, "I'm keeping this forever."

Sims

Chapter 26

Sinners Circle

"Everything happens for a reason," Marcy speaks, big chunks of green pickle mashing between her teeth. "You have to understand that God has a plan for each of us. Amanda, do you believe in fate?"

I turn off the tap, grab a dry dishtowel and throw it over my shoulder. I stare into the water, the thousands of tiny soap bubbles slowly bursting one by one. "I do and I don't."

Marcy fishes a big pickle out of green jar between her legs. "How's that?" She crunches hard into it, juice spilling all down her wrist to the elbow; I imagine we're two mad men out in the forest, starving to death and losing our minds from eating poison mushrooms. And then the day before we both die, I am naked and covered in mud and it is morning. And I turn around, fresh wind chilling my face, I see Marcy high out of her mind, eating frogs, their blood sprays everywhere.

I smile and she trails off. Our eyes meet and she smiles back. She says something about my mom as I wonder if there could ever be a frog with slimy bones. Firm slime, that's thickened its self, through various genepool collisions within nature, having stood the test of time throughout evolution. And it stood in the dark, alone with the bats and stared into nowhere. Lost in the abyss. All alone in an echoing cave where the temperature never rises.

I fish a fork out of the bottom of the sink and slowly rub it with a wash cloth. "I think we change things about ourselves that others do not like. And we think that we change for, what we perceive to be, the better. I think this is why there are so many problems. People get to thinking about themselves too much. Vanity is an obsession. And modern culture grooms us into narcissism. I think we're doomed to fail, as a species. I think us just being us *is* fate. Our actions are just a reflection of what we are meant to be biologically. But our actions and behaviors in themselves, that isn't fate at all, that's just *us*."

She takes another bite of her pickle. "Have you lost your mind?"

I press the fork into my thumb hard enough to leave a deep impression, then I drop it on the towel next to the sink. "I think we've all lost our minds."

"Well," She turns her wheel chair towards the *Last Supper*, a fresh one. She's started over. "*I* believe everything happens for a reason and that God is up there watching us and watching *over* us. Keeping us safe and away from the evil in this city." She points a paint brush towards the TV. "You tell me you aren't blessed, your mother whispering in God's ear keeping you safe in such an awful place as this. So close to that dreadful park full of ungodly people and human monsters." She points at the TV again. "Seen the news lately?"

"Well... sort of."

"Women are going missing left right and center. Police narrowed the search to right over there." Her paint brush aims out the window towards the park. "Right over there in the park. Joggers. Some ugly man is snatching women."

I squeeze two under water handfuls of cutlery. "Have they found any bodies?"

She fishes around in the jar between her legs, pulls out a giant toad cock and chews away half. "Nope. Not one."

"No bones or anything?"

She keeps chewing. "Nope. Nothing."

"Then how do they know the girls are even dead?"

"Dead? Who said anything about dead? If you ask me, it's the Mexicans. I think they're coming in over the border at night time and stealing white women and selling them into the sex trade. I'm not sure, but I've got a pretty good feeling about it." Toad dick grinding in her teeth she hisses in a whisper, "Sometimes, Francis comes to me at night. Sometimes, I can hear her tell me things. And I *do*—I *listen*, and Amanda, she is *proud* of you. She says there's a man in your life who will change *everything*. She told me this. *You'll see*." She winks and bites off another mouthful of frog sausage.

Chapter 27

After work, Sophie came over. Even though we'd been sleeping together, we still put the brakes on and decided it was best, well *she* decided it was best, that we got to know each other first and felt it out. I held everything in, I didn't say anything real about myself and what I didn't hide, I lie about everything. *But* this is a new chapter in my life. I want to move forward. She doesn't need to know about problems from the past. Problems that I can get rid of, if I have the right support. Like a loving girlfriend, who is normal in every way.

After about a month of this 'getting to know each other' nonsense, she was *mine*. And I never missed a single opportunity to tell her how happy I was about it. Well, I'm not good with words really. My mind is free but my mouth is sealed.

So, I do things for her to *show* her that I care. Like, we go for ice cream or a long drive. I showed her shortcuts. But mostly, we spent a lot of time together, at home. It was heaven.

I even introduced Sophie to, Marcy. Just not as my girlfriend.

Most nights, if she wasn't working late, Sophie slept at my house but it was getting more and more clear to me, especially after having met my aunt, that Sophie wanted us to spend more time at her place. I listened for subtle hints about us moving in together. I was prepared for it when it came again this morning.

My plan was to wait until Marcy died, then burn the house down. Collect the insurance, or just bulldoze the place and never sell the land. *Then* I could move away.

But the more Sophie talked about it, the more I came to see that Marcy could have a care worker and I could lead my life the way I choose. I thought about the basement. I thought how quickly I could dismantle everything. Not on a microscopic level of course but, just replace this, add that enough until the naked eye couldn't catch any cause for concern.

I didn't necessarily *have* to be here. I just wasn't ready to admit that to Sophie yet.

I was in love with her to the brink of obsession but I kept a cool demeanor and tried not to think about melting into her.

Tonight, I'd admiring her vagina as we lay on the bed. I'm kissing it and then pulling away. I'm stroking the lips and sucking on it.

Sophie hits me with a pillow and bucks her hips a little bit. She says, "What are you thinking about?"

I stroke Sophie's silky lips. I remember the time Blaine was telling me a joke about a guy who was so horny he runs downstairs to fuck a fish but the fish turns out to be a piranha. I thought that was really funny. I kiss Sophie's tiny pussy and then climb on top of her. I remember this joke I heard once, "A Thai woman runs into a wall. What does he break? Her boner."

I laugh and close my eyes. As we kiss my heart skips and folds, it detaches from my chest. It free floats through my entire body.

I pull away and she looks at me. I switch off the light and mute the TV. I tell her I love her because, I do. I kiss both sides of her mouth and we make love in to a blue midnight.

Chapter 28

Sinners Circle

It was Friday the 13th and Karl wanted to see a DJ at *Chambers*. He was moody because *Mystery Science Theatre 3000* went off air last week. We used to smoke pot and eat junk together while we watched it. I use the video tapes he gives me sometimes, to tape my girls on.

Alison was there, some pair of really wild eyed French Canadians had followed her here from another club. I don't like crowds, I hate crowds really. But I like to look cool, I like to think that maybe if I lead a normal life in some ways, those normal day to day things will bring me out of whatever mess I've been up to. *Oprah* said once that she saw a miracle in people who were really depressed but then they changed tiny little aspects of themselves and eventually, those tiny changes lead to other changes and before she knew it, she was in a new dress on *Oprah* telling everyone what to do.

So maybe, if I come to *Chambers* more often, one day *I'll* be the one on *Oprahs* couch.

I nod silently to myself and then order a drink. The place is still pretty empty. I'm surprised by that actually. Growing up I was always told faggots and gay people were evil, dark and constantly drinking alcohol and fucking each other. I thought that sounded pretty good. So, you can understand my disappointment when I came of age, only to step inside the red and mirror walls of *Chambers* to find, absolutely nobody here.

There's a trans person off in the corner by themselves. I can't tell if it is a boy or a girl, though. I don't care really, but it's always interesting to see the mash up. Like sometimes they're guys but with tits, sometimes they have collars, dress like women but have hairy everything. It's always fun. But to me trans people don't really count as human beings. Personally, I

Sims

feel a woman could never truly be a man. Despite mind set, despite any mental or emotional rationale. Women don't understand the world of men, the silent world of the dominant sex. They've entirely missed out on an essential time period during infancy. Social situations, society standards and our evolutionary instincts that hone a man through adolescence to manhood are not strictly biological. Deconstructing that vital and necessary community among men will lead society into a more emotion based sense of government. Which will weaken us in the eyes of our global enemies and ultimately lead to war. Which will fail, because we've sent a bunch of ladies with skin ripped off their arms and folded into a penis between their legs, go tripping over their boots in war. Not to mention morale decline among the ranks, with all this emotional horseshit every five seconds. Yeah, we'd all be dead on account of gross human error. Too many exit routes directing away from personal responsibility.

    I think it's kind of funny, in an ironic way, three tiny letters, DNA, would spark such a bitterness among the mentally deformed, as to form LGBTQ. I heard they're adding more letters. People are coming out as children now. Yeah, grown-ass adults. They wanna come to adult rallies to support their immersion into the community. Eventually they'll be messing around in parks. Yeah, some forty-two-year-old man is gonna be shitting their diapers in the sand next to your two-year-old daughter. And you'll think it's perfectly fine. Because all the weird faggots of the world got together and formed an alliance and made you let them dress up like dogs and play fetch with each other. They'll do it with guilt. I'm worried that it's only going to get worse. Because Christian ma and Christan pa are gonna fuck. And a whole bunch of little idiots are gonna tumble out of em soon afterwards and those little shit heads are gonna hate their parents because the parents have no idea what they're doing. They got married because they wanna fuck. Now they got a hundred babies and those babies are gonna grow up in rainbow Nazi, fagged-up environment; where everyone is stood in front of a mirror and told they're special.

Chromosomes. That's what determines gender. DNA will beat LGBTQ one hundred percent of the time. But, trans people don't get that. Trans people think whatever you feel is whatever is real. That's not okay. That's delusional, that's *dangerous*. However, I don't *really* care about trans folk though because like I said, I don't really think they count as people. I'm just saying, I hate how trans people will ignore science and reason, and just believe in nonsense because they can't get it together enough to just stop being fucking weird. It always starts as kids wearing wigs and leads to them snipping their dicks off with nail clippers at Christmas. Simply because they can't take responsibility for shit and that's why a lot of them go to jail as well.

    I walk over to the dark corner and stare at the trans. I drink beer and don't say anything. I think it's a girl that was once a guy. I kinda like that. I'd totally fuck a tranny.

    I tilt back my head and taste beer swill around my mouth. Then I purse my lips and shoot a slow fountain of beer into the trans face. I laugh a little when they flinch, and some gets in their eyes but, they aren't moving. Yeah, they just stood there taking it. They are statue. I laugh again. But then I start to worry that maybe they are a statue and maybe I'm hallucinating. So, I do it again and then again and I was about to do it again when I notice they're crying. I sigh, totally relieved as beer spills out of my mouth, washing down my chin and into the neck of my t-shirt. I sigh, totally relieved.

    I'm not crazy. I am sane.

    Their air dripping wet, we make eye contact. I'm grinning ear to ear. I say, "I'm sorry!"

    I walk back to my table and shrug. "Yeah, trans's are alright."

    I slide back into my seat. One of the French girls is talking and I can't really understand her. I check her breasts before deciding to move any closer to her. I do and I crane my neck like I'm listening. I like the perfume scent that rolls of the neck of healthy young women. At twenty-one, a woman enters a period of absolute physical perfection. Their vaginas are sweeter, elastic and pink. Totally fresh. I own a t-shirt that says that. Nobody knows what it means except for me. I love it.

She doesn't seem to mind my presence, but then again, her head is turned away and she can't see me. But I'm assuming she can sense me.

I make out they're discussing the solar eclipse in Europe and Asian and are asking each other why the eclipse didn't show over here in America. The chubby one with the nose ring and stretch marks mumbles something about a tabernacle.

I blink, pale and worm boards in a bowling alley flash through my mind. I'm an infant and I'm powerless.

I move away from the French Girl but I'm still watching her tits. I drink my beer and tap my fingers against the bottle. How fun would it be right now to have a dad who I could call from a payphone outside the club? He'd wear jean jackets and always talk about Led Zepplin. He'd kind of be like Tomm Chong but a lot older. And he'd be divorced from my mom, who would also be alive and we'd be really close but my dad and I would have a secret bond that made me feel completely safe and cared about.

I laugh. I get that same rush that happens when it's Disneyland on Christmas. And I'm rung up the ladder to perfect laughter, soul squeezing bliss. Angels kiss. And all the sudden I'm back again, in this body, in the here and now and I remember, everything is okay. I am safe, I am on the path of a brilliant life. A fantastic tale pushing the boundaries of imagination, the skin that streaks the complexion of the human condition. You don't need to understand. Acolytes. All of you.

Across the table I poke Karl. I lean over it. Things fall over. I don't care. I say, "I'm leaving."

He holds up a finger, like he does when he wants to say 'wait an hour?' when the music is too loud. I hate when he does this. It's dismissive and really puts me in a mood. I fucking hate Karl.

I smile and wave to everyone. I'm just about to use the bathroom but I see a crowd of people gathering around the trans, hugging them and getting a towel.

I head up the stairs and onto the street. I breathe the night air as I hail a taxi. The driver is talking on the ride home, but I'm not listening. I'm thinking about being on *Oprah*. I'd say "Now, *I am* the one in charge. Now everybody listens to me!" And I would tell all my favorite jokes and be the star of a TV show. Which I would set on fire, on live TV. I'd come in dressed like a real snob, then start shooting. Shooting everybody until the alarms are pulled, the sprinklers are on and the cops are coming. Then I'd blow my brains out like, Christine Chubbuck.

The Drums pound heavy. Everything is orange, everything is nineteen eighty-seven. Friday night, neon lights and black parking lots. Crimped hair, milkshakes and big plastic earrings. I'm so drunk, I pass out on the floor the moment I close the front door.

Chapter 29

Sims

I think I'm reading *Entertainment Weekly,* but I don't know. All magazines look the same.

I'm reading a review by David Browne about rapper *Eminem*'s single *Role Model.* David describes *Eminem* "...he gleefully debunks the idea of rappers as heroes..."

I smile, nod and put the magazine down. I trace my fingers over the buttons on the cash register. A large, thumb of a man, is standing there. Across the counter, jaw hung and gawking. My eyes move slowly across his facial features.

I swallow my gum. "Can I help you?"

He breathes through his mouth and his breath reeks. "Do you have any chocolate flavored lubricant?" My eyes follow his hands as they drop a crumpled package with: *Rubber Male Ass* blazed across the side in chunky yellow letters.

I wipe my hands on my smock. "No." I spent all morning movie boxes out of Blaine's office. I was covered in dust.

He just stood there, breathing like a Walrus in a heat-wave. He said, "Can you go check in the back?"

Having spent all morning moving around inventory, all the new stuff goes into Blaine's office for inventory count. I know for a *fact* there isn't any chocolate flavored lubricant back there. So, there's no need for me to check. I say, "We don't have any."

This Hot Walrus just stands there. Breathing and huffing and choking and being too fat. He's angry. He growls, "I don't want ass without the pudd'n!"

I laugh because it reminds me of *Pink Floyd* 'if you don't eat your meat you can't have any pudding!' I feel a warm wash over me, nostalgia, sunshine with mom. How we are all fated in one way or another to suffer in a way we cannot compare accurately with one another. How we're all in a personal hell, bricked away. How it all starts in childhood, how the system is corrupt and we are essentially the blind leading the blind. The time with mom, is so perfect. Then it all falls apart. Innocence shatters on impact and the shards are ground to sand. And that sand is pushed into the soil and parted by snakes and worms.

The Walrus chuffs. Sneering straight at me. "Well, it's no wonder you're the one in this equation wearing an apron." Then he leaves the store.

Swallowed by *Bush* kicks on the radio. Blaine approaches, wiping sweat from his forehead, eyes like a deer in headlights. "I'm worried to death about Y2K!"

I owe the album *Razor Blade Suitcase* I picked it up at HMV two weeks after its release in ninety-six. The album is amazing and what songs on the album that didn't quite match the masterpiece singles, remained legitimately iconic in the glory aspect of grunge that allows for incongruence. To me, Kurt Cobain is the father of all grunge music and I am faithful in my devotion to Nirvana but, *Razorblade Suitcase* **is** the album of the nineties.

To begin any decent review, I will not begin with any reference or comparison to *Sixteenstone* or *Glycerine*. It's too obvious a choice because it's everybody's favorite and that would be cheap and easy. There's nothing cheap and easy in Gavin Rossdale's work on *Razorblade*. However, it was producer, Steve Albini who really put the hours in behind this album. It's a shame really, and very telling of this world and her ways, how so many people who are talented and dedicated, *loyal* and hardworking... so many of them go unappreciated.

Swallowed was released in October of ninety-six as the lead single from the album. It dominated the US billboard for seven weeks, holding in at number one. I feel the weeks within that time frame were sacred. We were true nineties. The nineties had an orgasm in nineteen-ninety-six.

Apart from reading an interview in *Spin* with Steve Albini, I tried to avoid reading any interviews with the band. So far, I've been successful. Many may call me crazy but, personally, I feel when a band comes out with an album and those heavenly verses are played through into grunge rock overtures, I like to listen to it alone, uninfluenced and in heaven. I don't want to be told what it means. I want to take it home, and infuse it to my soul.

I feel it would be awkward and deeply disappointing to meet Kurt Cobain or Gavin Rossdale. Because their music is a honed assemblage of their art, polished and approved by multiple agencies. By the time it reaches the listener it's been so picked apart and combed over by standard commissions and record producers that, it's nearly an entirely different song. A lot of artists complain about that. Kurt did all the time. Isn't that how punk started in the first place?

So, I feel that in person, the artists themselves have got to be a complete mess. How low and horrible does your life have to get before you're able to make something beautiful? Kurt screamed so loud the whole world heard him. We knew him and we loved him. How loud can you scream?

But I digress, and I feel the fact albums are so torn apart by various agencies and departments, once again brings *Razorblade* producer, Steve Albini into the spotlight for his tremendous efforts to work *against* that and forward with the albums integrity.

Coming home, pressing play to *Swallowed,* I am instantly immersed by Gavin's gentle croon, "Warm sun feed me up, I'm leery, loaded up, loathing for change and I slip some boil away..." And them *bam,* I'm in. I'm under his trance. We slide so easily into the chorus we don't even notice. It's so natural, like slipping into a warm bath. By the second verse, I'm air drumming, I'm kicking chairs and my soul is ringing. Like an ethereal worm of light, love and understanding thrashes wildly somewhere deep inside me.

I always almost cry when Gavin confesses, "...and I'm a simple selfish son." But I find strength in his return to the chorus.

'Gotta get away from here...' Makes me imagine an exit. A turn in the road. And there, I'm a million miles away from myself here and this life. I start over. I'm a good neighbor, I help people. I do normal things and I'm okay, I'm alright. Gavin pours his heart out, "I miss the one that I love a lot." And I think "Mom." And I think of wheat and blue skies. Cotton dresses and a wrecking ball. Soil and bare feet. Crickets.

And then I turn it off and leave the house.

"Amanda?" Blaine is standing in front of me tapping the counter with a pen. "*Amanda*!?" He's chewing gum, his hair streaked back. He's got terrible skin and dark, eerie eyes.

I don't even blink. I just turn my head to him. "What?"

He says, "Did you hear what I just said?"

I didn't say anything.

He shook his head, "Goddamn, Y2K up my ass. I'm not good with computers either, like I said *don't worry about it*. There's some old dive comic shop down the street, a weird fat guy opened up after his mom died. Used his inheritance, always fucking with store owners around here. I hear he shoplifts as well." Blaine crosses his arms. "I know you don't know what he looks like but, when I see him I'll point him out to you. I need him to install updates it says or something, whatever. Fuck it."

He walks back to his office and I stare at the carpet for three hours. No one comes in. No one goes out. I parked in the front today, while I was walking toward the door, I noticed the sign facing me from inside the store said *OPEN*. My heart thumped in my chest. I power walked out the door and looked at *CLOSED* facing all who passed. My head shot up and I saw Blaine standing in the shadows, at the back of the store. I bit my lip. I shouted, "Just turning the sign! Have a goodnight!"

He didn't say anything but he raised an arm to wave bye. I closed the door and locked it. A cool wind bit into my face. I wasn't wearing a jacket. I had left it inside, on a at the back outside Blaine office. I put it there earlier while I was moving boxes. My teeth began to chatter. I looked in through the window into the dark of the store. The wind blew again, tossing hair into my eyes and mouth. My teeth chattered, biting into my hair. I imagine myself being eaten. I stand there with my teeth chattering, staring into shadows. After a minute I decide to leave my jacket because I have the car keys in my pocket.

I listen to Corey Hart's *Sunglasses at Night* as the horizon fades to pink, staining passing clouds and singing birds, purple. I wind down the window and put my elbow up. I slip on sunglasses and burn down the highway with the wind in my hair.

Chapter 30

"Do you want to go see *American Beauty* this weekend?" Sophie is stroking my hair. We're in bed, my head on her chest. I'm listening to her *heart beat.*

I open my eyes, and watch her close her legs. Her knees barely touch at the center. I feel the sheets on my skin, I'm cold all of the sudden. Clocks tick clicking like chalk crumbs hitting the floor, A cool snap flicks my beating heart.

Arthur Schopenhauer once said, "In a world like this, where there is no kind of stability, no possibility of anything lasting, but where everything is thrown into a restless whirlpool of change, where everything hurries on, flies, and is maintained in the balance by a continual advancing and moving, it is impossible to imagine happiness. It cannot dwell where, as Plato says, *continual Becoming and never Being* is all that takes place. First of all, no man is happy; he strives his whole life long after imaginary happiness, which he seldom attains, and if he does, then it is only to be disillusioned; and as a rule he is shipwrecked in the end and enters the harbour dismasted. Then it is all the same whether he has been happy or unhappy in a life which was made up of a merely ever-changing present and is now at an end."

I close my eyes, and breathe. Sophie still strokes my hair.

"So, guess who came back to the ward babe?" She tickles my cheek and smooths an eyebrow.

I smile. "Oh God... no way..."

She giggles then strokes my hair, "Yup, Mama Mildred Geef. Says she was enjoying recovery at home with her friends and family, wandered out by the pool and *bam!* She slipped and hit her head. So, third comma this year. Last year it was only two."

I laugh and roll on top of her. I love when she tells me stories about work. I love to imagine my beautiful girlfriend using her brain and being amazing.

I'm admiring her nose when she leans in and kisses me. I melt entirely. I even start crying. Sophie is so great, she doesn't even laugh or anything. She wipes my tears away but that only makes them come even faster. But I don't sob. None of that sobbing business. I can't stop myself from tears sometimes but, I draw the line at sobbing. That I *can* help.

Yeah, so what, sometimes I cry when my girlfriend kisses me. Fuck you.

I'm not always the best at expressing my feelings, I know that. But right now, it feels so *natural* beside her. *With* her. These feelings erupt when I'm near, Sophie. I worry constantly that I will scare her away. But I never do, and she never criticizes me when she can tell I'm distressed or upset. Her calm reactions at me are soothing. Her nurture is intoxicating, her love makes me drunk.

She smiles and laughs silently for a second. She pats the bed beside her and I lay there. "I swear to God babe, she's probably set a record. Stacy from downstairs is her nurse and she told me in the break room today that, Mama Geef queefs in her sleep!"

"That should be a bumper sticker."

Sophie is laughing, her face is rose red. Because I love talking to her about work, we kinda have this private soap opera that we're making up, gossiping about the people she works with. She told me about Mama Mildred and how she was constantly going into commas for weeks at a time. About three weeks was her longest comma. I even made a rhyme up about her:

> *Mildred Geef has gone to sleep,*
> *she'll wake again within a week,*
> *she snores all day, wears sores gone gray,*
> *No one visits! No one stays!*

Sophie doesn't like it. She says it's mean.

She shifts her body on the bed, draping an arm over my stomach. "The actor who plays *Roy* in *This Boy's Life* is in, *American Beauty*."

Sophie knows my second favorite movie is, *This Boys Life*. My number one favorite movie will always be *What's Eating Gilbert Grape*. I think Leonardo DiCaprio is going to be a huge movie star. In my eyes, he's already a living legend.

I kiss her lips and my heart flutters. "Yeah sure, I'll go."

When Sophie is asleep, I slip out of bed and stand in the basement. I look at the mulch remains of a woman I killed. Only a few months ago, this pile of offal was a living, breathing human being. I kneel down and taste it with two fingers. It's bloody disgusting but, I swallow anyway.

Schopenhauer said, "Looking at the matter a little closer, we see at the very outset that the existence of inorganic matter is being constantly attacked by chemical forces which eventually annihilates it. While organic existence is only made possible by continual change of matter, to keep up a perpetual supply of which it must consequently have help from without. Therefore, organic life is like balancing a pole on one's hand; it must be kept in continual motion, and have a constant supply of matter of which it is continually and endlessly in need. Nevertheless, it is only by means of this organic life that consciousness is possible."

My hands fumble around a bone and I weep until I think of something funny and start laughing.

I feel better.

I head back upstairs, get into the shower then back in bed with, Sophie. She snuggles into me and I kiss her forehead then fall asleep.

Chapter 31

It's October and I'm at home, watching Flinstones, eating a *Toblerone* I stole from a grocery store.

Barney and Fred are being tricked by the Great Gazoo again. But all I can think about is the first verse to *Oh Me* by *Nirvana*. I sing it in my head until I can feel myself drooling.

When I look up, TV says possibly thirty people have been killed in west London. It says, two trains crashed into one another in Ladbroke Grove. I turn off the TV and sit motionless.

Did you know that if the sun disappeared we wouldn't know for eight minutes? That's because it takes light eight minutes to reach earth. Then all hell would break loose and the suns gravitational grasp on our planet would vanish, along with the light. Then the earth would be shot into a straight line. Even though photosynthesis would stop, the earth would be fine because of the thermal vents inside the ocean.

The earth would just travel in a straight line until obliterated by something or caught inside the gravitational pull of another group of planets.

To me, this is really exciting. I think the biggest tragedy in life is that it's so short. We never really get to see anything change. We're alone for a really long time.

But mostly I just want to die. I like life but, from a distance. I find everything so fascinating, I can experience all the things that other people can experience but, I don't belong. I don't have a home place, an emotional destination. I have loss and anger. I am, profoundly, *alone*. Life and TV, there is no difference. I can never tell who is real, me or you?

I am an invisible. A tourist. I am, nobody.

My actions have no consequence; therefore, I do not matter. My 'victims' though, everybody says *they* matter. Everybody makes a *real* big show of that. Those girls will never be forgotten... or so their parents keep saying every six months or something on the news. I saw this one mom saying how she can feel that her daughter is still alive and asks the man who took her to please 'just bring our daughter home to us!'

I remember really rolling my eyes at that one. Goddamn slut pup, go have some more puppies.

Honestly, what the hell am *I* supposed to do about it? Show up at the cop shop, holding up a glob a slut slop like 'hey, this is five different chicks!'

And then what? The cops toss her teeth in a shoe box and rattle 'em at the mom like, "here's your dead kid's cavity ass teeth."

No, no. That would be rude. It'll blow over. Time heals all wounds. In two years the mom will get her daughters face tattooed on her shoulder and that will be that.

Maybe she'll be on *Oprah*!

I'm feeling better. I turn on the television. *Korn*'s video *Blind* is on MTV. The video sucks but the music is incredible and if you close your eyes you can really hear it the way it was meant to be listened to.

I don' t like the video because I think, David Silveria is a dickhead. Because he doesn't put any effort into dressing up like all the other members of the band. Yes, they look ridiculous, like adults dressed up as fifteen-year old's who dressed up for Halloween. But at least they're trying.

I turn off the TV and sit in silence.

To be fair, who *actually* drives me nuts is, Head. The bass player with baby hair and massive skull. The reason I don't like him is because, he reminds me of this dickhead from high school who used to listen to Dokken all day and talk about his dad. He said, every morning his dad gave him a pack of cigarettes said he had to sell them to kids for a dollar each and not to bother coming home till he sold them all.

His name was, Dale and he was in the same detention class as me because he got caught stealing Twisted Sister records from a car in the parking lot. I don't remember why I was in detention. I might have kicked in a door or something. I used to do that a lot. I went through a phase. I was always kicking down doors that looked loose.

I hated Dale because I saw him crying once when *Against All Odds* by *Phil Collins* came on. He just seemed like such a poser, his favorite bands were always changing and when I asked him if he liked *Pink Floyd,* he didn't know who they were.

Dale thought serial killers were really interesting and used to tap me on the shoulder and be like 'Want to hear a list of five of the worst ways to die?'

Even though his breath stunk, I said yes.

He was always talking to me and one day, all the sudden he started walking my route home. I hated that because I remember eating a lot of dog cum back then. Almost every day after school I would walk around the neighborhood, finding male dogs and beating them off. I remember being terrified I'd be caught and I was once but, I couldn't stop myself. I have very compulsive behavior and an extremely explosive sex drive.

But, when a horse nearly broke my jaw, I stopped swallowing animal cum.

I remember one day, after detention, Dale started walking home with me. He was talking about Ted Bundy and saying how he wanted to cut his English teacher's head off.

I don't remember the exact detail but, he followed me around for a bit and thought because he really liked messed up stuff he wouldn't care about me beating off dogs and so I ate some cum from a terrier and Dale ran away calling me every name he could think of.

It sort of turned me on that he knew how disgusting and polluted I was. How totally unnatural and *wrong* I had just acted. I think it was around then that I started putting dog shit inside me too. Anything really, even geese shit on the grass in the park. I'd scoop it up and carry it around inside me until I got cramps and laid down in the school nurses office after I cleaned myself out.

That's why I don't like people who think serial killers are interesting. Because they don't *really* understand what they're talking about. I'm not a serial killer. I'm an angry, damaged human being.

People get this idea that serial killers don't have feelings. And in the time they spend imagining their lives changing, via murder, they always go about killing someone in their thoughts that they think deserves death. Especially women. Women have no imagination when it comes to murder. It's always some victim-esque horseshit, some rape revenge plot somehow. Or some yellow-bellied Black Widow after the life insurance.

Men, the motive is sex. A quick fuck, kill, bury. In whatever order. It doesn't matter.

What frustrates me is, these serial killer enthusiasts conjure some idealistic scenario where their murder serves as a sort of edgy act of vigilante justice. I hate that. A serial killer is completely different. A serial killer is alone, angry, bitter and perverted. The overwhelming sense of loneliness and rage becomes too much. Nobody wants to be alone forever.

I feel like I've been alone forever.

I don't want to feel alone anymore. I need a complete release.

An audience is required. An audience under my complete control.

Fans of murder never think of afterwards. They don't realize the complete emptiness after the death rattle. The release has been had. Now, look what you've done.

But her body is still warm and her head isn't bloody if you turn it. She is a still presence. And I'm not alone anymore. Someone is here and she smells like somewhere else and it takes me somewhere else. I imagine what her home looks like, family coming over for holiday dinners.

And then her body gets colder and colder. Her skin, tighter and tighter. This always does it for me. I don't want to sound weird or anything but, I'm really into tight skin on dead girls. Drives me wild. No hold barred.

Disneyland on Christmas.

I can peel the skin off her body like wrapping paper. Then I take the toys out. If I swallow them, then she is mine forever and with me always. I always swallow them.

I close my eyes and smile warmly as I pat my tummy. I think of birds and yellow cotton. Sunlight and white fences.

I think of the full moon and the warm rain. I think about Sophie and I feel my chest cave in.

I hop in the shower then drive to Sophie's place. The moment our lips connect at the door, I feel her soothe me to my core.

I slip my arms around her waist, and study the feature of her face. I say, "I love you." And I mean it.

Chapter 32

I'm closing. I'm counting the coins and bills, I'm writing down the numbers and dividing the figures of the amount of cash in the till. Somewhere between the digits and their decimals something rings. I look up from the sheet of paper and towards the direction the sound is coming from. It's the telephone in Blaine's empty office.

I just sit there staring at a wall of pornography, then I drop the pencil and follow the noise. I stand outside Blaine's office door hoping the caller will hang up. But after the fifth ring I try the doorknob. It's unlocked. I watch the little red light on the phone turn on while the machine takes a message in silence. The waste bin, it's been emptied. All that's in there now are a few small balls of black tape rolled into bb's.

I sit down in his wasted looking swivel chair, fit my fingers together and close my eyes. I think of Sophie and how much I can't wait to squeeze her tonight.

I open my eyes and rest my elbows on the desk and sigh. I pick up the telephone, red light blinking on *New Message*. I dial Sophie, she doesn't pick up at home. I call her at work. Switch board connects me with the psychiatric unit.

"Hello, Psych, this is Mrs. Karen speaking."

"Hi, this is Amanda Troy, I'd like to talk to Sophie Harris, please."

"Who?"

"*Sophia* Harris."

"Just one moment, may I ask who I am speaking with?"

"Amanda."

"Who?"

"Amanda Troy."

"Ok, so an Amanda Troy wants to speak with Sophia Harris, I can pass on the message and who can I say is leaving the message?"

"No, this *is* Amanda Troy."

"Oh, sorry, that was a little confusing. And who do you want to speak with?"

I tap my finger over the flashing new message, covering and uncovering the light, watching it glow through my finger. "I want to speak with Sophia Harris, please."

Sims

"Oh sure, one second please. Sophia is just on her break. I'll put you through to the lunch room."

I hear Mrs. Karen put the receiver down and say to one of the other nurses, "How do you transfer a call to the staff room again? I keep forgetting."

A distant voice says, "I can't remember either, let me ask Michelle."

I shake my head and wiggle the mouse on Blaine's computer to see if he's got solitaire. His computer desktop, its total chaos, he's got files and folders scattered everywhere over a swastika background. I start clicking random folders seeing if anyone of them will pop up with a games menu or something.

Whoever Michelle is, she comes into the room on the other end of the phone and I hear her say to Mrs. Karen, "Oh, here I'll show you, just push..." then my phone beeps and I hear it ring onto another line.

I keep clicking folders, opening and closing them, dozens of porno JPEGS popping up all over the place. The line keeps ringing, the pictures start turning into animals fucking and being fucked, women roped up and bleeding, old people strapped to torture devices. He's got pictures of pigs being stabbed, burned and beheaded. I start closing the windows and pictures but stop when I recognize the shoes at the feet of the person holding the shank.

These pictures all have dates on the side. These pictures didn't come off the internet.

I click back onto the photos of women, bound and bawling, whipped and weeping, the same set of shoes as the others. I go to close the folder but wind up clicking on another one.

The phone picks up on the other end and Sophie says, "Amanda?" as I'm staring at hundred of pictures of myself in thumbnail size. Sophie says, "Amanda is that you?"

I click on one at random, I'm drinking a coffee walking to my Jeep after work.

"Amanda?"

I click on another one, I'm outside *Chambers* hailing a cab with the blonde waitress I killed.

"Amanda, are you there?"

I'm in the window, washing Marcy's dishes.

"Amanda, are you ok?"

I bite my lip and my heart stops beating because, I'm holding Sophie's hand in the park behind my house.

"Sophie... is Karl there?"

"What?"

I'm stabbing that grocery girl in the throat with a screw driver.

"Sophie, I need you to listen to me *very* carefully. I need you..."

Telephoto lens, I'm fucking Alison.

"Amanda, what's going on?"

Achromatic lens, I'm dusting dirt off my hands onto my pants as I look down at a grave I've dumped a body into.

"I need you to tell me if Karl is there."

"What? Why would you call me and ask that why didn't you ask if he was..."

Sophie and I, last night, kissing on the steps of her house.

"I'm coming to get you. Meet me in the parking lot."

"What? No, I have three hours of my shift left! What's this all about, are you cheating on..."

"*Sophie! Parking lot!*"

I hang up the phone and click on the last picture in the folder. It's dated same as the one of me and Sophie kissing on the stairs. It's dated from last night except one hour later. It's Marcy, hogtied on the floor of my cellar, her eyes scooped out of her head, her neck cut so rough, it looks sawed apart.

Everything goes blurry, the whole room spins so bad I fall off the chair, bang my head on the desk and throw up in the waste basket. My guts clench hard and deep into themselves but no matter how hard I shut my eyes or pull them open I can't get the picture of Marcy out of my head. Something falls off the desk and smashes me on the head. It's a camera, black tape over the flash, little pieces of tape over the little orange light that blinks every time you take a picture. I wipe a strand of vomit off my lip. I pick up the camera, peel off the tape, hold it close to my face and slowly roll it into a tiny ball. Drop it into the garbage.

I breathe, I stand, I go to walk out of the room, but that little red light flashing *message* catches my eye. I pick up the phone again, press play. A man's voice says, "How many tapes do you have? We'll pick them up in the morning; if these are fakes we're taking your balls *and* our money back."

I don't notice I've run a red light until someone plows into the back of my car. I stumble out, my forehead bleeding, the driver in the other car yelling after me, "Stop! *Stop!*" But I don't, I don't stop until I've ran the last five blocks to the hospital and my lungs are burning acid inside my chest.

Sophie rushes over to me as I fall to my knees panting in the parking lot. "Amanda! Holy Christ! What happened to your head? Come in the ER, I..."

I swallow air in gulps so fast I have to fight to keep from passing out, "Sophie, where's your car?"

"What?"

"Where's your car, come on." I wave, totally winded, away from the hospital. "We gotta go."

"What? No! We're going in here to get you some help, your bleeding all over the place it's..."

I shake my head and wipe blood out of my eyes. "No, you don't understand, I..."

"Did you take something?"

I stand up, reach in her pocket and snatch her keys. She tries taking them away from me, I grab her arm and twist it. "You're coming with me. This place, it isn't safe."

"What the fuck? Let go of my arm!"

"No, listen, you don't..." I take a deep breath and pull her towards her car.

She screams "Help!"

I let go of her arm and cover her mouth with my hand. I drag her in between two ambulances. "I'm *not* going to *hurt* you!" I check around to see if anyone is looking, there's not a soul in sight. "Just listen to me, you have to get out of here *now*. Someone is going to hurt you, really *bad*."

Her little arms go limp, she looks at me like I'm crazy. Like I've just broken her heart. She looks at me like she's actually seeing who I really am. I throw my arms around her, "Sophie, please just trust me, ok? I'm not going to hurt you, I would never hurt you! But I've done some things and I'm scared. I'm fucking scared that these things are going to take you away from me! Please, just trust me! I won't let anything happen to you."

I pull away from her, kiss the lips that pressed themselves all over my body in the shade of her bedroom last night. But my heart it breaks completely when I look into her eyes, brimming with tears, and the whole side of her face is covered with my blood, rolling in big drops off her chin, staining her white shoes. I slip my fingers through hers. "Sophie, I love you."

"I love you, too. Please, come inside, I don't care what you've done, let me help..." Her words are warm, but her eyes tell me she's lying. Her training is kicking in.

I grab her arm, push her towards her car and she screams help, I cover her mouth and drag her. I open the door and push her into the car, climbing into the drivers side. "You're coming with me Sophie. You don't get it *do* you? Do you think I'm fucking *joking*? Do you think I'd come here bleeding and screaming because I'm in love with some dumb fucking bitch and I can't control myself? Like I'm so fucking crazy about some dumb cunt I just met and I just *haaave* to see you because you're just *sooo* incredible and ..." She huddles into the window, I lean over and shout in her face, "... *blah blah blah?*"

I shake my head, start the car and light a cigarette. "Get your fuck'n head out of your ass." I wag a finger between us. "All *this*, I'm fucking saving your life."

She doesn't say anything and neither do I until we pass my car, all smashed on the side of the road, police cars and fire trucks blocking one of the opposite lanes. Sophie points, "Hey, isn't that your..."

I blow a mouthful of smoke out the window, shake my head and sigh. "Shut the fuck up."

"Hey! Don't fucking act like that! You don't get to show up and act like a fucking psycho without any explanation and not at least tell me where the *fuck* we are going!" She looks around out the window. "Hey, where *are* we headed anyway?"

"My house."

"Why?"

We stop at a traffic light, I slump my shoulders and rest my head on the steering wheel. "We have to go to my house for a couple minutes. I have to get some things." I reach for the cigarettes, tap the pack around in my hands. "Then we're going out of town to a motel."

"A *motel*? Are you crazy? I have work in the morning."

I sigh, rub my head, it's still bleeding, but not as bad. I can tell because it's not getting in my eyes anymore. "I'll explain everything. *Everything*, I swear." I pop a smoke between my lips, unlock the doors. "I don't want to force you or anything, you're free to..."

She snaps the door open, I grab the back of her shirt, yank her back in the car just as the light turns green and we drive off. She slaps my arm away "Hey! You said I could *go!*"

"Yeah, well, you're not supposed to."

"What?"

I light my cigarette, shrug and squint at the road with my good eye. "One of those *test* things that people do when they're in love. And *you* my dear..." I give her a wink. "You *failed*."

She shakes her head. I laugh. "Amanda, this isn't cool with me. I'll give you till we get to your house but, I deserve an explanation."

"True. And all people get what they deserve, right?"

"What the fuck? You think I deserve to be fucking *kidnapped*?"

"No, no, no. That's not what I'm doing. I'm saving your life."

She rolls her eyes and says to the window, "Oh right, *that's* what you're doing."

"You betcha'."

"You know, what's so great about you huh? Why do you think you're such hot shit? You're not, you're cold diarrhea. I see people like you *every* goddamn day."

"No you *don't*."

She looks at me, then back out the window. "*Every goddamn day.*"

"Sophie, look, you're right. You're totally fucking right. I am a total piece of shit, I'm not debating that with you. And I know this all looks, sounds totally fucking crazy, but trust me ok, please just *trust* me. I love you, I'm sorry I hurt you, honey. I'm fucking *scared* right now and I need you to see that and *understand* that and just *trust* me. If there's one thing you *ever* trust me with, it's this *one* time. Baby, please?"

She doesn't say anything, just bites her nail and stares out the window. We stop at another traffic light and I unlock the doors. She looks at me, puts her hand on the handle. "Would you really let me go this time."

I nod. "But I don't want you to."

She pops the door a little, "Amanda, is it really *that* bad?"

"Yes."

"Do I really need this in my life?"

"No. But I *need* you in mine."

"Are you going to tell me things I don't want to hear?"
"Yes."
"And if I don't like them, you'll let me go without hurting me?"
"Yes."
"Okay." The light turns green. She closes the door. "I'll go with you tonight."

I push the car into drive and roll through the intersection. On the side of the highway a bum is holding a sign 'Repent: The End is Nigh'. I close my eyes and see Marcy, scooped out and cut up. I gag and swallow whatever comes up. I look over at Sophie, she's clenching her hands together but her knees are apart. I'm not sure how to read her body language. I look at the cigarette between my fingers, my hand is shaking. I toss the butt out the window and feel my forehead. It's stopped bleeding but it aches, my whole body aches.

As I pull up to my house and kill the engine, I know that tomorrow I'll have to find some way to keep Sophie in the motel while I come back to burn it down.

"I'll just be a sec. Wait for me please?"

She nods, I'm about to pocket the keys but she leans in and kisses me. "I'm not going anywhere without you." I leave the keys in the ignition and get out of the car. I walk to my door, look back, she's looking at me, scared but smiling. I open the door and close it behind me.

I'm used to being alone, in all the years I've been here and brought someone back, killed them and kept their quiet corpse locked up somewhere, I've never felt it feel so empty as feels now. I don't have to know Marcy is dead in the cellar to know that she isn't here anymore. The vacancy of the building is loud and besetting.

I walk into my bedroom, everything is as it should be. Nothing's been moved or misplaced, it's all exactly the way I've left it. My clothes are still on the floor, until I pick them up, stuff them in a bag from my closet. Under my bed, all the photographs and Polaroid's of the women I've chopped up are still in their shoe box.

I carry the bag of clothes into the kitchen, walk to the couch, lift the cushion to see if anything important might have slipped under there. Then I walk back into the bedroom and throw some clean underwear. the sound of footfall above me, descend the stairs connecting Marcy's floor to mine.

"You think you're *so* smart, *don'tcha?*" Blaine stands in front of my couch, arms crossed. "*So* fuckin' *clever, don'tcha?*"

I can't even look at him. He steps closer in the dark. "You think you're just gonna do whatever you *like* huh? Hurt whoever you want and it *doesn't* matter, because you're so fuckin' smart they'll never get ya. You think you're in so much pain and you're so fuckin' badass killing women, huh?" He laughs, "You ain't shit."

He leans in the doorframe, chewing another huge wad of gum. "You think everyone else is pretty stupid, huh? Think you're putting something over on us?"

"Blaine—"

"No, fuck you Amanda Troy. Fuck you and your little miss serial killer *bullshit*. You know why bitches always get busted when they start *killing* people? Because they start fucking up, they start coming to work with blood under their fingernails and all over their shoes. They come to work reeking of death. You think you're a *monster?*" He shoves a thumb into the fat in his chest, "You're among the wolves now. I can smell you from here. People who don't know that smell, they just chalk it up to bad hygiene. But you ain't shit, except one sad little piece of dirty pussy that needs a good ol' fuck!" He thumbs his chest again. "I'm the big bad wolf, baby; I can smell a rat like you a *mile* away."

I back up, he doesn't move. "Ya know, at first I thought, gee maybe she's just nuts. But your buddy there... Karl, he came over one night when you were out bangin' that hooker bitch in your car." Blaine shrugs, "Yeah I got that on camera, made some good coin from it. Anyway, your buddy, we got to talking, told me some interesting stuff he's found around your place while you're all fucked up and wandering around the park with your face painted white..." He points to my bed. "...like a fuckin' junkie. Yup, found some video tapes. Did you know we're pulling in fifteen grand each little episode of yours? We sell 'em to the weirdos and kid fuckers in town here. Lord knows what *they* do with them."

"Blaine..."

"No, no, let me finish please. See, we got to thinking, if there's a market for *that*, well, what about the bodies? There's no sense in wasting them. So, we got those too. We sold them in parts, skeletons and junk, human body parts will go for quite a bit of dough, so we didn't mind if you ate one or two, because the cash would come in anyways. So, we waited, we waited and waited and kept getting more and more money from your little shenanigans. Thing is though, Amanda, when Karl told me about your little girlfriend..." He backs into the kitchen, looks out the window, "...is that her? Gee, she's pretty."

I slam my elbow into the window, grab a shard of glass and run at him. But he's faster and punches me in the face, stomps on my chest and slices my hand open wide as he pulls the glass from my fist. "Karl told me about that little bitch of yours, and how you started acting like a doe-eyed dyke. We couldn't lose our little investment because *you* think you're in love." He laughs so hard he starts coughing, "Seriously, Amanda, look at yourself. You're not a person, you're a *monster*. Look what you did to all those people. Look what *you* took away from *them*. They were happy and in love, and you *took* that from them." He laughs and slaps me across the face. Hard. "Now you want me to let you *live* because you think you found love? You did this to *yourself. You* did this. So, you tell me little girl, *you* fucking tell me why *you* deserve to live after all the lives you've ruined and stolen and the hearts you've broken. What makes *you* so goddamn special, huh?"

He kicks me in the ribs hard enough for me to hear them crack. "So, what we're gonna do is we're gonna sell those tapes. We're gonna sell those weird fuckin' pictures under your bed and we're gonna cut you up. You and lesbo lady over there in the car, and we're gonna see you in parts. How's that sound?"

He steps on my wrist, dips a finger in my blood and licks it off. "But *you*, I think I'm gonna fuck that little pussy of yours first. I mean, once you're dead."

Karl walks down the stairs, shotgun swinging at his side. "Oh hi, Amanda."

Blaine looks at Karl, "How about it? You hit her mouth while I hit her cunt?"

Karl smiles, brushes some of that fag hair of his out of his face. "Hell yeah!"

Karl opens the door walks outside. "Heya Sophie!"

All I can hear is her screaming, even when Blaine pulls me by my hair out the door onto the lawn and up against the house. Even when Karl bends over, waves at Sophie and blasts straight through the window, firing twice, all I hear is her screaming and it blends and echoes into a choir of women roped to the chair in the cellar, my mother weeping at the hands of her murderers. I don't see Blaine take a revolver out of the back of his pants, but my hands go up like I don't want him to shoot. And when I do see and he does shoot, I really don't hear or feel the bullet pass through my ring and middle fingers. I see them in slow motion, floating away from the others. And it doesn't hurt when my cheek burns hot, or when my teeth slip down the back of my throat or explode in my sinuses.

I don't feel any of that. I don't see any of that. But what I *do* see is the thunder storm forming in the summertime. And what I do feel is the breeze of the weeds blowing on the back of my knees. And what I *do* hear is my mother's heart pounding as we rush through the wheat before we're captured as thieves.

Sims

Made in the USA
San Bernardino, CA
23 March 2018